"Oh, Anna. How incredible that you've come back,"

Garrett whispered, touching her cheek.

She could feel his breath on her face as he leaned toward her. His finger shaped her lips as his eyes followed. His body was strong and warm against her. His lips were gentle on hers, soft, tempting. He tilted her head to taste her deeply.

And then, abruptly, reality intruded, demanding that she understand what was happening. She stiffened and pushed away from him, away from the feelings that flooded her. She met his look of surprise with a flash of anger.

"Is this part of my job description?" she asked hoarsely.

"What?"

"If you want me to work for you, then this can't happen again."

"Just business."

"Just business," she echoed.

But that would be easier said than done...

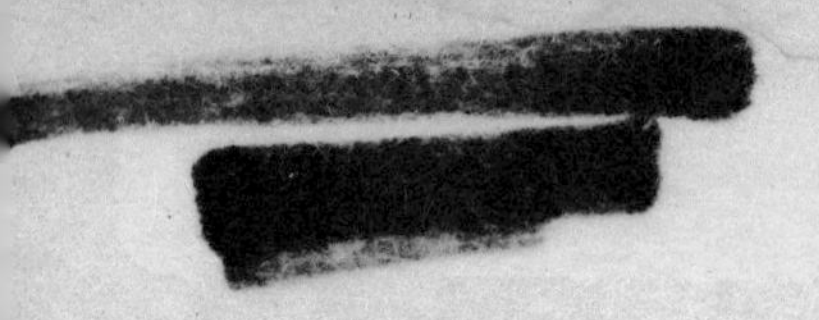

Dear Reader,

Welcome to the Silhouette **Special Edition** experience! With your search for consistently satisfying reading in mind, every month the authors and editors of Silhouette **Special Edition** aim to offer you a stimulating blend of deep emotions and high romance.

The name Silhouette **Special Edition** and the distinctive arch on the cover represent a commitment—a commitment to bring you six sensitive, substantial novels each month. In the pages of a Silhouette **Special Edition**, compelling true-to-life characters face riveting emotional issues—and come out winners. Both celebrated authors and newcomers to the series strive for depth and dimension, vividness and warmth, in writing these stories of living and loving in today's world.

The result, we hope, is romance you can believe in. Deeply emotional, richly romantic, infinitely rewarding—that's the Silhouette **Special Edition** experience. Come share it with us—six times a month!

From all the authors and editors of Silhouette **Special Edition**,

Best wishes,

Leslie Kazanjian,
Senior Editor

GRACE
PENDLETON

Heartstrings

Silhouette Special Edition
Published by Silhouette Books New York
America's Publisher of Contemporary Romance

For Emma and Marc
with love

SILHOUETTE BOOKS
300 East 42nd St., New York, N.Y. 10017

ISBN: 0-373-09579-1

First Silhouette Books printing February 1990

Printed in the U.S.A.

GRACE PENDLETON

spent eleven years in the Pacific Northwest before moving to Connecticut, where she teaches reading at a private school and tries to keep up with two active children and a physician-musician husband. An amateur musician and actress herself, she writes during every spare moment.

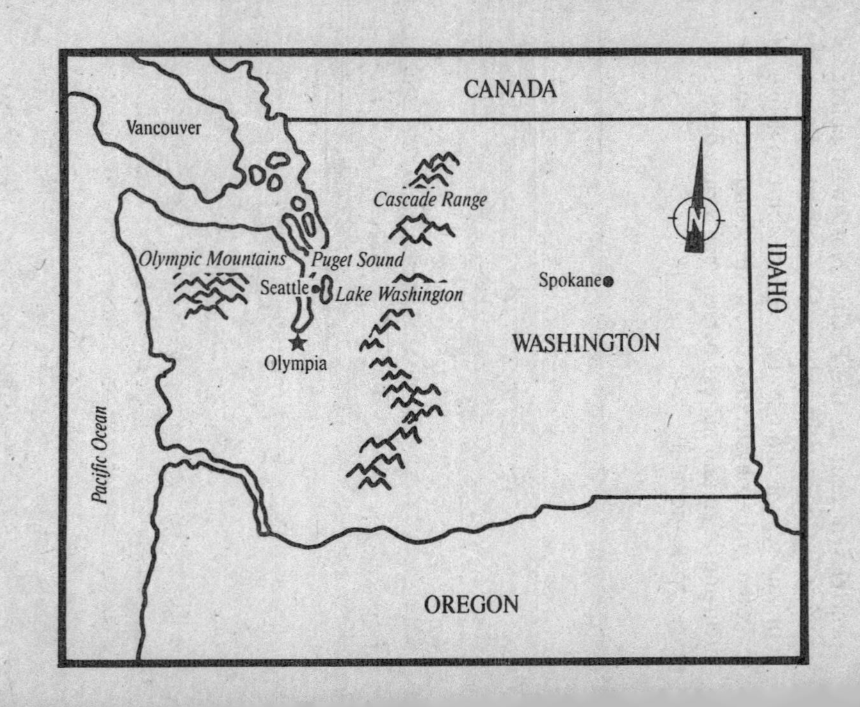
CANADA
Vancouver
Cascade Range
N
Olympic Mountains
Puget Sound
Seattle
Lake Washington
Spokane
IDAHO
Olympia
WASHINGTON
Pacific Ocean
OREGON

Chapter One

She wanted desperately to tell the bus driver he didn't have to hurry, but the big bus was already careening down Denny Way well on its way to Seattle Center. She wanted more time to think. More time to wonder why on earth she was putting herself through this again.

At twenty-five Anna Terhune was the possessor of a violin five times her age, a master's degree, several serviceable long black skirts and a great deal of determination. For eight of those twenty-five years she had lived in Boston. For six of the eight, she had studied hard to win her degrees with honors. For the last two years she had worked hard just to be able to keep playing music.

In graduate school she had played for the sheer joy and love of it—practice sessions, recitals, orchestra concerts, chamber concerts, late-night jam sessions. But once she'd won her degree, Anna discovered real life: playing music to pay the rent. She held down two small-paying jobs in suburban orchestras; she played with a trio at weddings and receptions and gallery openings; five afternoons a week she taught children how to play the violin. But when she added it all up, and added the total to the meager sum left from the inheritance that had purchased her education, it came out the same: insufficient to sustain life.

Everyone had agreed it was time. Time to take auditions. Time to try to get a full-time job with a real full-time orchestra that paid its musicians real money to play real music.

Auditions were a grim and terrible reality that faced any musician who hoped to make a living by his art. The trade paper advertised them every month, and everyone had horror stories about them and oodles of advice on how to deal with them.

Once she'd made up her mind that winter, Anna, in typical fashion, proceeded to devote herself wholeheartedly to the task. She wrote and rewrote her résumé, had it professionally printed and sent it with a letter to a dozen orchestras that were each looking for one or two superb violinists. To the eight that replied favorably, she sent a professionally recorded tape of her playing, and waited. Six responded with invitations to audition and told her when and where to appear and what to play. Three auditions took place in the East almost immediately. The other three took her to the West Coast in May. And the last of these would be at the end in this crazy bus ride through her old hometown.

Seattle, Washington. She'd left eight years ago and simply never gone back. Both parents dead, she had only two ties to the city: her father's sister Claire, a potter who lived in a peeling Victorian house across from a park, and her old teacher, Simon Weil, the retiring concertmaster of Seattle's Northwest Symphony Orchestra. *Retiring* was the operative word. Anna's teacher was retiring and his old student, somewhat aghast at her own temerity, was on her way to try to take his place.

She'd arrived in Seattle on an evening flight the night before, and no Aunt Claire had dazzled forth from the crowd. She'd called her aunt's number to find that the woman was the same as ever. She was in the middle of a "delirious teapot" and advised Anna to "take a cab, dear, and let yourself in." This was the same aunt who had come all the way to Boston for Anna's graduation, then gotten waylaid in an art gallery and "lost track of the time."

The bus lurched and Anna cradled her violin case protectively on her lap, leaned her weary head against the smudged glass and stared with horror and fascination at the shifting skyline. It wasn't really like coming home at all. How could a city change so quickly? It wasn't a comfortably low-profile dowdy little town anymore, with only a few tentative skyscrapers. In eight years Seattle had sprouted fantastical shapes and mirror-windowed monoliths.

She was grateful the sun was out as she squinted against the brilliance. On its sunny days Seattle had always resembled a gaudily tinted postcard, and it certainly had on its Sunday best this May morning, its greens and blues taking on a fresh new identity. When she'd phoned her Aunt Claire to tell her that she was finally coming for a visit, Anna had only requested one thing, a few days of perfect weather. Despite being absentminded, Claire apparently had friends in high places. Not only was her aunt's lavender rhododendron out in all its splendor, but it looked as if the entire city of Seattle had exploded overnight into summer.

Anna closed her eyes and in her imagination let herself rise birdlike above the city. To the east she saw the residential hills tip into the long azure expanse of Lake Washington, and even greener hills climb out and up in random heaves toward the snowy peaks of the Cascade Range, visible this morning from Mount Rainier in the south to Mount Baker in the north. And to the west, between and beyond the futuristic towers and vast reflective surfaces of the New Seattle, deep blue Puget Sound spread north and south, tastefully dotted with white sails. Beyond the sound lay Bainbridge Island and beyond the island rose the Olympic Mountains. Defined by water and mountains, the geography of Seattle was sharp and resolute.

Anna opened her eyes and her mind veered abruptly back to the task at hand—her audition scheduled in forty-five minutes at Seattle Center, home of the Northwest Symphony. She could see the Center now in the middle distance, the Space Needle rearing its fanciful flying saucer in its midst. Unconsciously fingering her violin case, she thought back to the countless trips she'd made to Seattle Center's Concert Hall as a teenager, all energy and confidence, in blue jeans, a sweatshirt and braids, with her head full of visions of concerts and standing ovations. This was entirely different.

This time she was dressed in a conservative navy suit with a white blouse and low-heeled shoes. She'd tamed the dark brown curly mass of hair that would run riot past her shoulders given the chance. It was all gathered in a firm knot at the base of her neck, and camouflaged combs secured the tendrils that would have liked to curl around her ears.

Two more stops to Seattle Center. She took a deep breath and held her hand up in front of her face. It was fairly steady, considering. A person needed to be a little nervous to do well. Just the right amount of nervous. The slight tremor in her hand looked just about right.

Everything counted this morning. Everything counted in any audition. A veteran now, she'd learned that lesson well. There were so many things to think about. It wasn't enough to have the proper credentials, the right recommendations, a terrific audition tape. You had to look good, carry yourself well and play like an angel. And it always helped if you knew somebody who could put in a good word.

Simon Weil. She'd called him last night, apologetic about being out of touch, concerned about his retirement. After assuring her that his only real problem was an aging body and a desire for a change, he listened to her tales of her previous auditions, her fears about the impending one and said finally, "Anna, you've got a chance. You wouldn't be here if you didn't. But you need to believe inside, inside yourself, that you can do the job."

"That's what's so hard, Simon. I hear myself and know I can do better."

"No. That's wrong. You have to believe in yourself, you have to have complete confidence in yourself when you walk in there tomorrow morning. You have to think, 'I am Anna Terhune. I am a great violinist. I am going to show them how great I really am.'"

Anna smiled into the phone. "Simon, you said that to me before my first recital when I was ten."

"It's still true, my dear. It's all in your mind. Your fingers know their business. Your ear knows its job. It's your mind that holds the key."

There wasn't an answer. Anna knew he was right. "Will you be there?"

"Oh, yes, I'll be there." The old man sighed.

"How many are auditioning?"

"Two dozen."

Anna was astounded. "Is that all? I thought there'd be at least a hundred."

"The fact is, there were well over a hundred applicants. Garrett screened every tape. But he did it blindly. He said he didn't want to know their names or anything. He just listened. He knows exactly what he wants. So you see, it isn't really such a . . ."

"Garrett Downing." She said the name softly. It wasn't as if she didn't know he was the conductor. It was just that she'd tried not to think about it.

"I think you'll find him quite changed, Anna."

"Well, I'm glad to hear it," she said sincerely, and made Simon laugh.

"He's always been a fine musician."

"I know that. But I can't say I ever got along with him too well."

"You were very young. So was he."

"Mostly he was impossible. Nasty. Rude. Sexist. Awful."

"He's mellowed."

"It must have been your influence."

He chuckled. "I take some credit."

"Well, he's going to have his job cut out for him, finding a replacement for you, Simon."

"I think he could do far worse than hiring you, my dear girl."

She took a deep breath and asked the question that had haunted her for weeks. "Tell me, Simon. Did I get asked to audition because of you? Did you ask them to invite me?"

"I would have if I'd had the opportunity, Anna," he answered in his forthright manner. "But as I said, Garrett labeled the tapes with numbers and said he didn't want to clutter up his head with résumés and credentials and letters of recommendations. He said he'd written too many of them himself to trust them. He came up with two dozen violins he wanted to hear again in person. Yours happened to be one of them."

"So he doesn't know he's invited me?"

"No. It's a little game he's playing. He wants to hear the auditions and decide if he can tell who's who."

It sounded so much like the Garrett Downing she remembered that she had to smile in spite of her misgivings. Garrett had been twenty-eight when he'd been hired to pick up the pieces of the Northwest Symphony Orchestra, a young, struggling, disorganized mixture of professional and amateur musicians. Born in England, a child prodigy who by fifteen had forged a reputation as a mature pianist, he'd turned to conducting in his early twenties and had moved to Seattle to take his first full-time job. It was a job he took very seriously.

Anna could remember her first glimpse of him that afternoon in March at a rehearsal of the Youth Symphony. She was sixteen. Running in from the bus, breathless, eager to meet this new conductor she'd heard so much about, she'd barged into the hall and been royally dressed down by a man with a nearly incomprehensible English accent for being five minutes late. Tall and thin, his reddish-brown hair overlong, his eyes perennially sardonic, Garrett Downing had taught her during the months that followed just how egotistical and demanding a conductor could be. It hadn't helped that he was alarmingly handsome and could flash her a smile that warmed her to her toes. Because in the next moment he could freeze her blood with a caustic word and make her wish she'd died a month ago.

Despite the fact that everyone had assumed that Anna would take over the position of concertmaster of the Youth Symphony that spring of her junior year in high school, Garrett Downing had other ideas. He announced he didn't believe in concertmasters for Youth Symphonies and had moved her all over the violin section. She once dared him to place her in among the cellos, and he had called her bluff.

Before her senior year was over she'd nevertheless played a lot of music for him and learned that his ruthlessness was tempered by a devilish sense of humor, that his impatience masked a meticulous attention to detail, that his passion for perfection was coupled with a wild enthusiasm for his work. Over the years since, she'd remembered the man and his passion and tried to forget the way her stomach used to knot at the sight of him.

Anna pulled the buzzer cord and got to her feet, hunching over to watch as the bus lurched to a squeaky full halt. With the ease of long years of practice, she expertly balanced her trim black shoulder bag, her leather music folder and her violin case and swung down the stairs onto the sidewalk. She turned automatically toward the concert hall. She wouldn't have to ask directions the way she'd had to in San Francisco. She could walk this part of the trip in her sleep.

Her heels clicked a steady tattoo on the sidewalk as she strode beside the high wall that enclosed the Center. She was beyond nervous now and even eager to begin. She'd have time to warm up and give herself a good talking to before the ordeal got underway.

She knew now that she'd come back to show Simon and the impossible Garrett Downing how much she'd learned, how far she'd come. She wasn't an ardent high-school girl anymore. She was an ardent adult with one passion: her music. And she wanted to show off. For the first time in many weeks, a genuine smile played over Anna's face. She wouldn't think about the job and the fact she hadn't a prayer of winning it. She'd play for the audience, for the sheer joy of pleasing them, the sheer pleasure of astounding them.

She pushed through the enormous doors of the concert hall and abruptly found herself in near darkness. The lobby loomed around her and its cool eddies of air made her shiver slightly under her wool blazer. She blinked to adjust her eyes to the gloom and saw ahead of her taped to a red padded door a sign reading Auditions—Quiet Please. Taking a deep breath, she squared her shoulders and went through the door.

A blond woman with tortoiseshell glasses and a pleasant smile greeted Anna and told her that the auditions were on schedule. Far away she could hear music, the warm thin sound of a single violin. One other person, a man, roamed restlessly at the far end of the room, dealing with his own nerves.

Anna found another corner, shed her blazer and unpacked her violin. These last moments of waiting were the worst, she'd learned that well enough. She tuned the strings and warmed up her fingers, playing softly, steadying herself as she climbed through the familiar musical passages. When she looked up again, it was in response to the woman calling her name.

She answered the flutter of panic deep in her chest with a determined lift of her chin and walked through the door.

A grand piano, shiny and black, stretched across one side of the stage. A middle-aged woman in a yellow dress sat at the keyboard, eyeing Anna with curiosity. A sturdy black music stand stood near the piano. Black curtains hung down on all sides, screening off the rest of the vast stage, hiding the auditorium Anna knew was there, filled with an unknown number of listeners. And in three straight-backed wooden chairs sat three men.

Simon looked smaller, his blue eyes paler, his halo of wispy hair whiter than she remembered. He gave her a confident smile. Next to him sat a man she didn't know. And in the third chair, his long legs crossed in front of him, his arms folded, sat Garrett Downing.

It was the man in the middle who spoke. "Number 089," he said, and Anna imagined it was for the benefit of all the people she couldn't see who were going to listen to her and judge her. Then he said, "089, First Movement, Mendelssohn Violin Concerto." Anna glanced at Simon, who winked conspiratorially and nodded, and then let her gaze pass quickly over Garrett, who simply stared at her.

She raised her violin to her chin, touched the strings and took a moment to tune up. Suddenly the waiting was over.

As the familiar notes emerged from her fingers, Anna felt a welcome surge of confidence and power. She was glad they'd chosen the Mendelssohn. It was technically challenging and deliciously lush. It didn't even matter that a single piano was replacing the orchestra. That was the pianist's problem, not hers. This was music she could really put her heart into. She closed her eyes and let her mind and soul dictate the music she poured forth.

There was no applause as she lowered her instrument, only silence. She looked first at Simon whose smile appeared to have frozen in place. The man in the middle made a few notes. But Garrett Downing was in motion. He stood and strode to the side of the curtained-off area, then stopped abruptly and looked at her. She watched his every move then took a breath to speak, but he raised his finger to his lips to silence her. She understood then that she was Number 089, neither man nor woman, neither young nor old. She waited.

"089," he said, "I'd like you to play something else now. Bach. Yes." He waved off the piano and pointed to Anna, adding, "Unaccompanied. Just you. Whatever you choose."

Amused but also somewhat reassured by this unorthodox behavior, Anna smiled politely. Dressed casually in a blue-striped open-necked oxford shirt and navy slacks, Garrett was still a slim six feet with a full head of dark red-brown hair that curled at his neck and ears and sent a wayward lock over his high forehead. His finely boned face was impassive, all angles and shadows in the harsh lighting of the stage. But his eyes gleamed with something like mischief as he gave his terse orders. His once-marked English accent now only shaded the corners of his voice.

She was prepared for this eventuality and held up two fingers, indicating the she would play the Second Sonata for Unaccompanied Violin by Bach. He nodded in comprehension and stayed where he was.

Anna then placed her violin under her chin and closed her eyes. For some seconds she was very still, gathering the notes in her mind, willing the sounds from the depths of her being. Then she began. Her wonderful instrument, a violin she'd owned since she was sixteen, its sound contained by the heavy curtains all around the stage, nevertheless sang sweetly in the space. Alone. No piano clashed with the golden sonority of the strings. Nothing interfered with the dense sounds.

Until a voice said quietly during a pause, "That's enough."

She jerked as if awakened from a dream.

"That's a dreadful thing to do to anyone," admitted Garrett Downing, "and I'm very sorry to do it. But I've heard enough. And any more would put us behind schedule," he added.

The only thing Anna realized coherently was that Garrett, Briton that he was, still said schedule with a *sh* sound at the beginning. In another few minutes she was outside blinking in the sunlight, wondering if she'd just had a dream or a nightmare.

The call came through to her aunt's house in the late afternoon. She was asked to come back, at ten o'clock the next morning.

"I'm in the final cut, Aunt Claire." Anna stood in the door of the studio, watching her aunt as she shaped a platter on the whirring wheel. Her voice was low with suppressed excitement.

"Of course, dear," her aunt declared. Claire was dressed in her usual potter's garb, an ancient long denim skirt and multicolored Guatemalan shirt. Her dark red hair lurched wildly in all directions, kinky with curl and laced with gray. Anna didn't have to look far to figure out where her hair genes had come from.

Anna shook her head in disbelief. "People like me don't get in the final cut."

Claire Terhune stopped her wheel and looked squarely at her only niece. "What does that mean?"

"It means what it means. I was a finalist in San Francisco but that was for a rank-and-file violin. Any old violin. Even that is amazing in itself. At my age. But this is totally different. I can't believe it."

Claire started her wheel up again and focused on her platter. "I can. It stands to reason. You're a Terhune."

Anna walked slowly back to the house. It was as if she'd never left. Claire was still the same offhandedly affectionate, distant, preoccupied aunt who'd always given her whatever love and attention she could spare. When Anna's mother had died in an automobile accident when Anna was nine, Claire had fussed over her for a while, then gone off to Central America for a year to study a specific kind of pottery technique. Alone with her father, Anna had done her mourning in silence, in solitary silence. Her father had hired a woman to care for the house and the child, and distanced himself emotionally from the grief he couldn't face.

Anna realized that, after all, coming home meant nothing. If she emerged from all the torture of this audition with a job offer and came back to Seattle, she would be starting from scratch. She wouldn't live with Claire. She couldn't even depend on Simon to smooth her path; he was leaving early in June and would be traveling all summer. As usual, she would find her own place and make her own way, alone. She shivered in the cool night, glancing back at the shed that housed her aunt's dreams and art. She'd never known anything else but solitude. Solitude and music.

She slept badly and woke to catch the same morning bus that had borne her downtown the day before.

She wore the same suit with a clean white blouse, feeling superstitious but secure.

The same pleasant woman was sitting in the lobby, and Anna went through the same ritual of warming up and preparing herself. This time when she emerged through the doors onto the stage, she saw the entire auditorium yawning wide before her. The piano had been pushed aside. A conductor's podium and music stand were centerstage, and next to it on one side stood a black music stand and a single chair. Final auditions, Anna had learned, were studies in controlled insanity. In a final audition, the conductor conducted a single musician playing orchestral music without any orchestra to help. It was one of the loneliest experiences in the world, and one of the most nerve-racking.

Anna's gaze swept the hall. There were people sprinkled all over the auditorium. A few in the balcony. Several in the first few rows. Simon about ten rows back, looking as if he were dozing. Time held its breath. Then abruptly she heard a rapid stride and Garrett Downing swept onto the stage from the wings. He was all motion and energy, dressed in pressed khakis and a burgundy rugby shirt with a white collar. His hair spilled about as if he'd combed it with his fingers.

"Here we are then," he announced. He stopped and sized her up, his hands on slim hips. His pale gray eyes leveled at her. "Number 089. Alias Anna Terhune." He shook his head, his mouth compressed in what might have been a grin. "My God," he murmured.

She met his look and wished he weren't quite so handsome. It wasn't just his looks, for his face was perhaps too thin, his straight nose just a little too long, his mouth slightly too cynical. It wasn't even his eyes, large and deep set, full of intelligence and life. It was his whole aura. He seemed to glow and gather clouds of electricity around him. As she looked at him, she found it in her heart to wish him fifty, bald and boring. "Yes," she replied evenly. "The same Anna Terhune you pushed around all those years ago."

He smiled, showing a glimpse of square white teeth. "Yes. But not quite the same." His expression changed as he took a breath and said, "Well, we'll let that pass. We've got some work to do. Glad to see you've brought all your music. You won't need it. I've got what we'll need right here."

He was on the podium, then off it again, thrusting a few sheets of music at her, putting the rest on her stand. He motioned her to take the chair while he jumped back up on the podium and rifled through the pages of his scores.

Once in her chair, she remembered to take a few deep breaths as she consciously relaxed her shoulder muscles and softly checked her violin strings. Then she waited, ready and alert, never taking her eyes off the conductor.

"Let's begin with Mozart," he said, naming a late symphony.

He waited while she found the specific selection and then, commanding her every nerve and muscle, brought down his baton. Anna did not listen to the hollow sound of a single violin playing a Mozart symphony, but instead concentrated on the music and Garrett's directions. After two pages, he brought her to an abrupt halt and looked over at her, an odd expression tipping his mouth. He raked a hand through his hair.

"Brahms," he said succinctly, and then named a slow section from the composer's first symphony that Anna knew contained a solo bit for the principal violin. Again, Garrett commanded and Anna willed her every muscle to obey. His single-minded concentration on her playing was only mildly disconcerting. In a real rehearsal or concert his attention would be spread over the entire orchestra. But not for this. He was learning how she responded to him, and she gave him everything she had to give. They played as a single instrument—he formed the music with his hands and body in thin air, she drank it in and translated the written notes and his gestures into pure sound.

Tchaikovsky followed the Brahms. Then Bach. Then Shostakovich. He stopped abruptly, midpassage and took a deep breath. Anna relaxed for an instant and became aware that her back and temples were damp with perspiration. She shifted a little in her clothes, but never lost her awareness of the man in front of her. The great hall was absolutely quiet, as if the two of them were all alone. He chewed his lip for a moment, and handed her a single page of handwritten music. It was a challenging piece full of difficult, shifting rhythms and rattling dissonance. As Anna played it she didn't even have time to be thankful she was good at sight reading.

The page and the music ended jarringly. She reached to flip the sheet over and discovered the other side was blank. He looked at her. "That's all I've had time to write down."

"This is yours, then?"

"What do you think of it?"

"I hate it." After she spoke, she wanted to bite her tongue off.

He barked a laugh. "That's the spirit. That's the way you played it. Tell me. Do you have any energy left?"

"Sure. This is what I'm here for."

He checked his watch.

"Your audition tape was Brahms's First Sonata." It was a statement.

"Yes."

"Do you have it memorized?"

"Yes."

"Come here, then." He was already moving. "Not the whole thing, mind you. I just want to hear a bit of the first movement."

They might have been completely alone in some living room. There might have been no audience out in the vast reaches of the hall. Garrett strode over to the piano and played some chords. Then he looked at her. She adjusted her strings to the piano and stood quietly, trying to gather the music in her head.

"Just the two soft chords at the beginning and you start."

"I know."

"You know," he echoed with a grin. But he waited until she nodded at him, and they began. If Anna had known when she awoke that he would have asked her to play a Brahms sonata from memory, she would have been a nervous wreck. But as it was, she just played the music. He played to her and around her and the music flowed effortlessly. When the piano stopped abruptly, Anna looked up, stunned.

"God, I hate doing that when it's going so nicely," he said as he rose from the bench. His eyes were serious, luminous, disturbing. "I'm sorry. But there's no point. I've heard what I need to hear." She hesitated. "We're all done," he explained. "You can go."

"But what now?" she managed to ask.

"I'll be in touch, Number 089. You'll hear something from somebody by tonight."

Chapter Two

At five-thirty that afternoon the telephone rang. Anna stared at it. She'd been waiting all afternoon, alternately hopeful and desolate, giddy with excitement and sick with dread. Now she wasn't at all sure she wanted to end the suspense.

"Hello," her voice croaked out.

"Anna?" His voice. She hadn't expected that. Yet, there was no doubt in her mind whose voice had just spoken her name.

"Yes."

"Garrett Downing here."

"Yes." There seemed to be no breath in her body. All her senses were reduced to a single one: hearing.

"Everything all right there?"

"Yes."

"You sound terrified."

A laugh erupted from somewhere inside her but died before it could surface. "I guess I am."

"Well don't be." She couldn't speak. "You still there, Anna?"

"Please, Mr. Downing. Just tell me if it's yes or no."

He actually had the gall to chuckle. "Can you be presentable in a half hour?"

"A half hour?"

"I'll pick you up."

"But why...?"

"To talk about this troublesome subject of yes or no."

Her mind veered around to the logical. "Should I bring my violin?"

"Only if you want to. Or if you don't have a safe place to leave it. But you won't need it. Perhaps you'd better tell me where you're staying."

Anna gave him the address and then replaced the receiver slowly, trying to make her brain work.

Her aunt came through the kitchen door at that moment, heading for the sink with her hands stained dark red with clay. Anna didn't know whether to laugh or cry. She couldn't even move. She waited for her aunt to notice her.

"Well, there you are, dear. Any news?"

"I just had a call."

"Well, about time. Good news, I trust." Claire wiped her hands on a ragged towel and plucked an old ginger cat from the counter on her way to the pantry to find it some food.

"I guess so." Anna shook her head. "I don't know. The conductor's coming to pick me up at six. He wasn't very forthcoming. But he wasn't negative, either."

A smaller black-and-white cat poked in from the dining room, purring. Anna watched Claire feed her pets and stroke them, murmuring, answering their purrs. Just as Anna was about to turn and leave the room, her aunt stood and gave her a direct look. "It sounds good to me," she said. "Sounds like they want you. So put a smile on, girl, and go act like you own the world. Right now you look about as confident as a wet kitten."

In another minute Anna was in the shower. Ten minutes after that she was slipping a teal silk dress over her head and pulling it down around her slim hips. She adjusted the cowl neck and checked her stockings for runs. She organized her hair in a sort of loose bun and applied a modicum of makeup. Her hands were shaking, and she mentally cursed Garrett Downing for being so mysterious. And for being a few other things that didn't bear thinking about.

The knocker knocked at five minutes before six. Anna dashed out of her room, down the stairs, took the turn too quickly and slipped on the scatter rug at the bottom. She caught herself, shoulder first, crashing against the front door and wondered bleakly whether he'd heard her. She gathered up her nerves and slowly opened the door. His eyes were wide and full of concern.

"Raising elephants in there?"

"I slipped."

A grin danced across his face. "No serious injuries, I trust."

"Only to my pride. I guess I was overanxious. Can't imagine why." She moved aside. "Come in. I just need to get a jacket."

He stepped over the threshold. "Who're you staying with?" he asked as he and the black-and-white cat surveyed each other.

"My aunt. Claire Terhune. She's a potter. I'd introduce you, but she's out back in her studio trying to turn out a complete tea set by next Sunday."

"Talented family."

Anna glanced at his face, but it didn't reveal a thing. "You know you're being very cruel about all this."

His eyebrows shot up. "Cruel?"

"Mysterious then. Maddening."

He shrugged and held her jacket for her. "Come, let's get on our way. We'll talk about it in the car."

The car was a small silver Jaguar lurking by the curb. She should have guessed he'd have a car like that. She decided to ignore it and pretend it was a Chevy.

They drove in silence down the street. Anna folded her tense hands in her lap and thought about relaxation techniques. Within moments Garrett was nosing the car into a parking place across from the Art Museum in Volunteer Park. From here they looked over the city and a lowering sun filtering through the leaves as it dropped toward the distant Olympic Mountains. He switched off the engine and turned to her.

"To begin at the beginning, I'm very curious about something. I want to know what gave you the idea that you could come here fresh out of school and audition to be concertmaster with my symphony." He clipped his words precisely and wasn't smiling.

Suddenly the smallish car seemed tiny. It was a question she'd given a lot of thought to, but was there a right answer? Or did it even matter?

She considered for a moment, then decided she had nothing to lose. She spoke carefully. "I didn't think of it in those terms exactly. It was a job. And I need a job. I wish it had been another position. Honestly. It's the only audition for principal that I've taken. Though, as you know from my résumé, I've acted as concertmaster for several orchestras in and outside school. As for being 'fresh out of school,' that's not strictly true. I've been studying the violin since I was five. The master's degree I got two years ago was just one more step." She wondered if she were just digging a deeper hole. "I guess I felt the audition would be a good experience. I felt it was a good time to try. Try for something that seemed out of reach."

"Did Simon advise you to apply?"

"No," she responded quickly. "Actually, I've been terribly out of touch with him the last few years. But he was definitely a factor. I could say I wanted to try for his sake." She paused. "I spoke to him the other night after I got here. He told me I had a chance." She looked over at Garrett. The sun was gold on his profile as he gazed out over the city. "Did I? Have a chance?"

"A mere girl. Barely twenty-five. No real experience at all." He turned toward her, giving her the full benefit of his smoldering eyes. "What in heaven's name made you think you'd be qualified to take Simon Weil's place as concertmaster?"

His voice had changed tenor; it challenged. She cleared her throat and said evenly, "Probably the same sort of insane reasoning that made you think you were ready to conduct a symphony orchestra when you were twenty-eight."

He stared at her for a second, then threw his head back and laughed. "Anna Terhune," he stated, as if listening to the sound of it. "Tell me this. If I did offer you the job, would you take it? There's the move to consider, across the country. All those boyfriends to say goodbye to. Three thousand miles to come with nothing at this end but a wall-to-wall schedule this summer that won't leave you any time for anything. Probably not even any breathing. And then there's me. You'd be working for me. Something you never seemed to enjoy back when you were in the Youth Symphony. So think very carefully before you answer."

"I wouldn't have auditioned if I weren't interested in the work. But I can't figure out if you're offering me the job, Mr. Downing."

He ran a hand through his hair, sending it into disarray. "I think I am. It goes against all reason and common sense. It even goes against my better judgment. But I want you," he said quietly. "Your violin. Your sound. Your musicianship. Your art. I want you in my orchestra. Actually, I'd like a dozen like you."

The moment froze. Her heart stopped, and the whole world seemed to whiten at the edges of her consciousness. The sensation lasted no more than a second and she found her voice. "You're quite serious."

"Quite." He offered her his hand. "Congratulations."

She was having a hard time closing her mouth and she ignored his hand. "Why did you just have me convinced five different times that I'd completely blown my chances?"

"I was curious to know how far your self-confidence went." He shrugged and added, "Pretty far."

"Why couldn't you just tell me over the phone?"

"Ah. Because it's not quite so simple. There are a number of difficulties. There's a certain risk involved...."

"Because I'm a woman?" she asked incredulously.

He smiled grimly to himself and let out a slow breath. "Yes, I'm afraid so. There are some rather traditional types on the committee who think you might not look the part. They wanted me to move the assistant concertmaster into the chair and be done with it, especially since..." He came to a full stop again and Anna kept quiet, sensing that he was gathering his thoughts.

"I may be the conductor. I may be the music director. But they do pay my salary, not to mention yours, and they think I've lost my mind. Because you're just the beginning. I'm making a lot of changes in the orchestra for this summer program, paring some sections, adding new people, new sounds. It's been a fight all along, and you're just the newest factor.

"Actually things were going well until yesterday. Number 089 walked out on the stage. I'd already decided that 089 had something nobody else did, just on the basis of the tape he'd submitted."

"He," Anna echoed.

He flashed a grin. "Right. So today everyone else found out. The point is the last person anyone expected to see on that stage this morning was somebody like you. It was upsetting. Unsettling. Amazing. Actually, it was a lot of fun."

"Well, if it's any comfort I couldn't tell what you were thinking."

"Do you know, Number 089, that women aren't supposed to play the violin the way you do?"

"It's been mentioned from time to time. And it always manages to sound a little insulting."

"Hmm," he responded. "I guess what I'm trying to say in my poor, feeble way, to put it bluntly, the problem is you're not a man."

"Isn't there a law against this now?"

"Now don't go and get legal. Look at my position. From your sound you're supposed to be middle-aged and internationally famous. A male. Goes without saying. But you're not. I want to hire you anyway. Regardless of age or sex or color or any of that. But the committee wants to interview you." He looked at his watch. "In twenty minutes."

She drew a breath but he cut her off. "They would have sat on this for another week or two. I don't know what your situation is, but I want this taken care of as soon as possible. There are ten other auditions coming up during the month and a vast quantity of details to settle before the summer."

Anna sat very still for a moment. In the past five minutes she'd been called a girl, a risk and a problem. But through it all was sprinkled not a small amount of left-handed praise, and somewhere in there she'd definitely been offered a job. Her mind was reeling with confusion.

His voice came through low and clear. "What it comes down to is you're going to be offered a three-month contract. A kind of a probationary status. Just for the summer season. The Seattle Summer Festival. It's something I've been trying to get off the ground for five years now. And you're going to be a key part of it. You're going to work harder than you've ever worked in your life. A real trial by fire. After three months, well, we'll negotiate. If we feel you haven't held up your end, you're out. And if you want to leave, you're free to go." He shifted in his seat so he could look at her. "What do you say?"

"I don't know yet."

"A cautious lass, aren't you?"

"Let's just say I want to know more about it."

"All right. Let's go down there and you can ask the committee all the questions you want. You can talk money and pensions and health plans until you're blue in the face. But don't you balk if they ask you if you're considering marriage or pregnancy anytime soon."

"That's ill—"

"I know it's illegal. But they might ask all the same. Just be tolerant."

Abruptly he pulled out of the space and wheeled through Volunteer Park. Anna was trying to get her thoughts in order, trying to sort out the kinds of questions she would ask, the sorts of things they might ask her.

"One more thing," he said, his voice intruding on her thoughts. "What are we going to call you? Master or mistress, hmm? I don't think I've ever heard concertperson."

He looked as if he thought the whole issue was very amusing. "In every other orchestra I've played in we've always just used *concertmaster*, Mr. Downing. And that's fine with me."

"Right. But you can call me Garrett. We Westerners are pretty informal about that sort of thing." She didn't want to look over at his grin.

The meeting was blessedly brief. An anticlimax after that strange interview in the small car. Simon's presence boosted Anna's self-confidence; Garrett's presence she tried to ignore. The manager explained about the three-month contract, and added graciously that he hoped they would be able to renew it for a full year in September. Anna agreed to take the job and appear the next day to sign the contract.

Simon, always gallant, kissed her hand. "So you see, Anna. You did have that chance." His thin white hair wisped about his head. His blue eyes were bright but tired. Now that she was standing close to him, Anna was shocked at how much he'd aged.

"Simon, I still don't believe it quite yet. I keep expecting to wake up."

"Will you still be in town tomorrow?"

"Yes."

"Let's have some lunch together. Like old times. Twelve at the Space Needle?"

"Let's."

Garrett walked up. "Well, Simon, you knew it all the time, didn't you?"

"I had my hopes." The old man smiled and winked at his former pupil.

"I smell a conspiracy," declared the conductor. "Garrett, take this child to dinner. She looks as if she needs a square meal."

"Are you hungry, Anna?" Garrett seemed astounded by the possibility.

"Yes, I guess I am."

"Will you join us, Simon?"

"No, but thanks. It's been a long day. And if I'm not mistaken, we have another long day tomorrow."

Goodbyes were said, and Anna found herself alone in the conference room with the man she'd just agreed informally to work with for the next three months. A man she'd just agreed to have dinner with. A man she was entirely too aware of as a man. She was suddenly sorry about the dinner.

"Look, Mr. Downing—" she spread her hands "—Garrett. You don't have to take me to dinner."

"You can buy if that'll make you feel better."

She smiled.

"Say, you do know how to smile."

"Listen, I..."

He cut her off with a gesture. "No, I understand. You don't want to eat dinner with your new boss. Perfectly understandable. The problem is we're both hungry. And I have to take you home, right? I mean, back to your aunt's. And your aunt is still working on her tea set no doubt, right? So you'd have to fix something yourself. And I'd have to go to my house and fix something. Isn't it easier if we just go to a restaurant and eat?"

She couldn't think of a logical argument and within minutes they were driving north toward the Shilshole section of the city. He'd ascertained that Anna had spent nearly forty-eight hours in Seattle without having salmon and decided to rectify the situation.

"Penny?" he asked as they waited for a light.

"Not worth even that, I'm afraid. I'm feeling a little stunned by it all."

"Tell me about your other auditions."

"I was in San Francisco Monday. I made the finals, but I won't know until the end of the week."

"Hmm. San Francisco. Good orchestra. Any others you expect to hear from?"

"No."

"Seriously?"

"Seriously." She told him about the other auditions and how she'd done. "Are you sorry now?"

"No. Don't be daft." He turned into a parking lot. "I know what I heard. I can't help it if no one else hears it. They'll hear it soon enough." He pulled into a space. "So what's wrong with the East Coast?"

"There's no real work. Just a lot of jobs. And New York is a zoo. Not to mention an easy place to starve in."

"So I've heard. I've conducted there a couple of times. And in Boston."

"I know."

"Oh, really?" He sounded genuinely surprised. "Which concert?"

"The one you did with the BSO. A Mozart overture, a Britten suite, Brahms's Fourth."

"Well, you didn't exactly let me know you were there." He frowned and glared at the steering wheel. "Perhaps I shouldn't have mentioned it."

Anna stared at his clenched hand on the wheel. The knuckles were white. Could it be that even egomaniacal conductors were human and knew moments of self-doubt? She hastened to reassure him. "I enjoyed it. A lot. You were very impressive. It was a very polished performance." Anna groped for words. "I actually did come backstage, but there were so many people. I remember thinking you made quite a hit. And then I had someone waiting. So... Well, anyway, I didn't think you'd remember me," she ended lamely.

Garrett gave her a quizzical look that slid away as he got out to open her door. He offered her his hand, which she took after only a second's hesitation. The car was low and her skirt was slim, and it was nice to have a little help for a change. Then she looked past him and her breath caught in her throat. He turned to see what had caused her reaction.

The sun had disappeared behind the Olympic range, throwing the rugged peaks into sharp black relief against the cloudless pink. Puget Sound lay still as a lake and reflected a fragmented sky from its gently bobbing waves. Bare-masted boats motored silently by out in the channel, and lights glittered weakly from the opposite shore. "It's so beautiful," Anna murmured. "I'd really forgotten."

"Ah. Wait until it's rained for seventeen straight days. You'll wish you were back in Boston. Or anywhere."

The view from inside the restaurant was enhanced by its subtle lighting. The maitre d' greeted them and showed them to a corner table by the window. It was an understatedly elegant place full of stained oak and white linen and well-dressed diners enjoying their meals. Before Anna could object, her companion ordered a bottle of champagne.

"Perrier's more my line, I'm afraid," Anna admitted.

"Not tonight, surely. This is a celebration. If I hadn't wanted to celebrate, I would have taken you to McTaco's."

She laughed, then smiled at the candle flickering in its glass bowl. She told herself she had to keep her balance. She was in new territory. She knew that she wasn't supposed to feel anything for this man on the other side of the table. But there was something undeniable coiled deeply inside her that made her every nerve aware of him.

"That's a rather nice smile, you know. You shouldn't be so stingy with it."

She raised her gaze to his and kept it steady. "Garrett. Don't you think it would be easier if you didn't try to flirt with me?"

"Was I?" he inquired innocently.

Anna gave an exasperated sigh.

He placed his hands on the table. His fingers were long and beautifully shaped, flexible, strong. "You're right, Anna. I honestly didn't mean to. I was just making conversation, just trying to put you at your ease, not the opposite."

He sounded so sincere that she relaxed just a little. She made herself meet his eyes. "Let's pretend that I'm a middle-aged male violinist of international renown whom you've just hired to be your concertmaster."

He blinked, then grinned. "Well, that sounds like fun."

And oddly enough, it was. For when the champagne came they toasted "Music" and Garrett's questions led her to talk about her teachers, her recitals, the orchestras she'd played with, the ones she'd heard. They talked musicians and composers, symphonies and sonatas.

"How's the salmon?" Garrett asked her when they'd exhausted the topic of the Julliard Quartet.

"Wonderful. They think Norwegian salmon is salmon back East. This is heaven. Perfect."

"Good. More wine?"

"No thanks. Any more and I'd slip under the table."

"I'd help you discreetly to your feet."

"I'm sure."

He shook his head in amusement. "Oh, Anna. Anna Terhune. I remember you, you know."

"And I you." She noticed the gleam in his eye. "But you go first."

He drummed a little tattoo on the tablecloth. "You were a spoiled brat. Sixteen? You didn't take anything from anyone. So serious I worried your face would break."

"*I* was serious? You were awful. You never let up on me one minute. I thought you were the spoiled brat. I hated you," she blurted out.

There was a pause. "That bad?" he asked softly.

"Sometimes."

"Well, I won't make you sit with the cellos this summer."

Then she had to laugh. "That would be nice. Simon told me you'd mellowed."

"He did, did he?" He had to think about it for an instant. "Perhaps I have. But I won't be easy on you. And for another thing, you'll have to make your peace with a section that doesn't want you."

"I was beginning to realize that at the meeting. I'd decided not to think about it until tomorrow."

"The work will make what you've been doing seem like a picnic."

"Are we really playing twenty-five concerts?"

"Probably more. But not as an orchestra. Just five as an entire orchestra. The rest in small groups. Quartets. Quintets. Trios. Duos. It all adds up to a lot of music. All over the state. So every little town has a chance to hear someone from the orchestra. Even if it's just you and me."

"You and me?"

He took a sip of wine and nodded. "Right. Sonatas for violin and piano. Several recitals, here and there."

"I didn't know you did that sort of thing. I knew you were a soloist once upon a time, but accompanying is . . ."

"Preferable actually. I've been playing quite a lot of chamber music lately. Especially this last year. I'd let the piano go a bit, but suddenly found the motivation to get back into it." He examined what was left of his own salmon filet for a moment. "When will you be coming back to town?"

"I don't know yet. I haven't really had a chance to figure out all the logistics of moving."

"If you can, try to be back by the last Saturday of the month."

"I'll try. Why that particular Saturday?"

"It's the gala. The very last concert. Of this season I mean." He hesitated. "It's Simon's last concert with us."

Something about his tone of voice made her say, "You'll miss him."

He didn't really answer her. "This has been a brutal year for him. He's been wonderful about it all. But it's been hard." He paused while the waiter removed their plates. "The gala has become something of a tradition. We program only the great war horses. The venerable favorites that people always seem to want to hear again and again."

"And this year?"

"This year we're doing Mozart's *Jupiter* Symphony, Mendelssohn's *Italian*, and Beethoven's *Emperor* Concerto."

"Who's the soloist?"

She saw the color rise on his neck. "You're eating dinner with him."

"Oh."

"Oh, as in have you lost your mind? Or oh, as in may I have your autograph?"

"Just oh. It's quite an undertaking." Beethoven's last piano concerto was a tour de force. That Garrett would attempt it as soloist and conductor told Anna quite a lot about his ego and self-confidence.

"Can you be there?" he was saying. "I'd like you to be. To hear the orchestra, you know."

"I'll try. I don't know how long the move will take."

"Rehearsals for the summer will start by the end of the following week."

"So you said. Don't you ever take a break?"

His gaze searched hers for an instant, then slid away to the little round candle holder. "Oh yes. Usually the last two weeks of August and all of September. If we live that long. Do you want dessert?"

She ordered decaf and he ordered coffee. She rested her elbows on the table and her chin on her hands. He leaned back in his chair. She knew he was watching her and she averted her own gaze out the window, searching the blackness for light, aware that mostly what she saw was their reflection, hers and Garrett's.

"You make me think," he said at last in a voice that rose as he spoke from softness to a kind of forced heartiness, "of a line in an Oscar Wilde play. It's when one of the women in the play meets another of the women and says she wishes that woman were 'fully forty-two and more than usually plain for her age.'"

She looked at him. "I can't help what I am."

"I know that," he said softly. He seemed to give himself a mental shake. "Well now, are you ready to go?"

The outside air was fresh and welcome after the restaurant. A path led off along the water under high arching willows trailing leaves pale in the lights reflected off the water. "How about a short stroll?" Garrett asked as he cupped her elbow.

"If it's a very short one. I've just about run out of steam."

They walked slowly in silence, the only sounds those of the gently moving water, distant boats and buoys, cars up on the road. He'd released her arm to walk next to her, but she felt the heat of him beside her, could still smell the faint hint of some musky fragrance. She thought about the quote from the play.

She knew what he was saying and suddenly liked him for saying it. She found herself wishing he were someone else. Someone not connected to this job, this new life. Someone who wouldn't be commanding her every living breath and musical sound over the next three months. Someone she could learn to know and care about. But they were who they were, and all the wishing couldn't change that. After this one evening they would have to go their separate, parallel ways, distanced by the same art that brought them together.

They stopped as if by one will. He pointed out the lights across the way and named the places to her as his other arm went round her shoulder. The weight of his arm was so wonderful, she knew she should move away from it. But she couldn't. She glanced at him to find him looking at her, his pale eyes shining, asking.

He touched her cheek with a finger. "Oh, Anna. How incredible that you've come back," he whispered.

She could feel his breath on her face as he leaned toward her. His finger shaped her lips as his eyes followed. His body was strong and warm against her. His lips were gentle on hers, soft, tasting. His hand spread against her cheek, caressing, urging. He tilted her head to taste her deeply.

It was like a dream, something she was a part of, yet completely separate from. It was as if she were watching herself from someplace nearby. She felt herself moving toward him, responding to him, and it was thrilling, fascinating in its newness. Then, abruptly, reality intruded, demanding that she understand what was happening. Astonished with herself, stunned by her own weakness, she stiffened and pushed away from him and from all the feelings that flooded her. For an instant he resisted, tightening his hold, but as quickly he released her. She met his look of surprise with a flash of anger.

"Is this part of my job description?" she said hoarsely.

"What?"

"Is this sort of thing buried in some clause in my contract? Because if it is, you can forget it."

"Do you think I . . . ?"

"I don't know what to think. But if you're planning to trade this job for sexual favors, you've got another think coming."

The moment's silence was charged. Anna was breathing in short, angry gasps. The muscles of Garrett's jaw bunched. And then suddenly his mouth smiled, an odd upturn that didn't include his eyes.

"I apologize, Anna. Blame it on the wine. Overactive hormones. Whatever. Obviously, I've made a mistake."

"Yes, you have."

His eyes softened. "You're a beautiful woman, Anna."

"That's hardly a compliment under the circumstances." She wished she could quit trembling. It was hard to steady her voice.

He seemed to weigh her words. "Perhaps you'd better explain the circumstances."

"You're hiring me to do a job, Mr. Downing. And you're also kissing me and telling me I'm beautiful. How in heaven's name am I supposed to do a decent job if I have to worry about compromising myself with you?"

Garrett ran a hasty hand through his hair and blew out a breath.

"I was foolish," Anna admitted. "I never should have let it happen."

"So where does that leave us?"

"That's up to you."

An expression flew over his face that made Anna's heart turn slightly. "Just me?" he asked.

"If you want me to work for you, then this can't happen again. No flirting or dinner dates or little innuendos. No kisses."

"Just business."

"Just business."

Chapter Three

The most difficult moments of the evening came during the ride back home. Sitting next to Garrett in the car, aware of his every movement, Anna felt terribly uncomfortable. The silence was leaden. It was impossible to think clearly. He had kissed her. A simple fact. She had kissed him back. That didn't work out as simply.

He spoke first. "Anna?" She couldn't answer him. "Are you still angry with me?" His voice was soft but tinged with roughness, and she realized with a little jolt that he must be as tense as she.

"No, not really angry. Just kind of confused, I guess."

"You were so quiet I'd decided you must be angry. I'm afraid you're deciding to turn down the job."

"No. I want the job. I just don't want the confusion. I don't want . . ."

"To be harassed," he finished bluntly. "I don't blame you. It was a thoughtless thing for me to do. I was totally out of line."

She couldn't say anything.

"It'll never happen again," he said.

"Then that's settled," she announced, hoping to put an end to it. She tried to smile at him, but it didn't quite come off. She was glad the car was dark and his eyes were on the road. She heard him take a breath to say more when she leaned forward, pointed and said, "It's the second house."

He found a parking place two houses down and maneuvered into it neatly. "I'll walk you back."

"It's all right. I'll find my way."

"Anna." He was offering her his hand. She stared at it an instant, then placed her own in his. His was warm and dry and closed briefly on her small cold fingers.

"Thank you for the dinner," she said formally. "And for the job."

"My pleasure," he said automatically. He raised his eyebrows. "You haven't changed your mind then?"

"I really can't afford to change my mind at this point. I need this job. Any job, actually. And I promise I'll work very hard. If you promise to keep your word to leave me strictly alone."

His eyes narrowed. For the first time since she'd challenged him, he seemed angry. "You have my word, Ms. Terhune. I have better things to do than chase violinists, believe it or not."

She was on Claire's front porch before she heard the car pull away. She was in her bedroom before a single tear leaked out. Angrily she wiped it away and collapsed in a slump on the bed. "Oh, hell," she whispered. "Why now? Why him?"

Morning brought strong coffee and a slightly better perspective. Anna decided that the entire episode had simply proven that they were both human. Garrett was only a man, after all, with the normal drives and passions. She was a woman with, she assumed, drives and passions. So their coming together was a purely physical thing. An involuntary act. Irrational, perhaps. Not unpleasant, but not something to be repeated.

She felt satisfied with this explanation as she rode the bus through a misty rain to Seattle Center once again. She looked forward to no stressful auditions or interviews this time. Just lunch with an old and trusted friend.

Simon Weil loved the Space Needle as if he had invented it. The first time he'd taken her to the restaurant that revolves at its top was for her tenth birthday. She'd felt very grown-up, she remembered, and she could still recall the dress she'd worn. Simon was already more than just a violin teacher to her by then. Her mother was dead and her father had buried himself alive in his work and grief. And Anna had been emotionally and physically alone. Except for her violin and her teacher. She had two lessons a week and lunch with him once a month until she left for college. But it had been a long while since their last lunch together.

The elevator, glass-sided and silent, bore her upward. Anna had to circle the restaurant once before she spied Simon. He was seated at an outer table, smiling and waving to her. He rose to salute her on both cheeks and then they both settled into their chairs.

At first Anna could only gaze out at the clearly defined mountains to the west and east. The city was playing peek-a-boo through the mist.

"Wasn't it clever of me to arrange this for you?" Simon was asking his delighted companion.

"I honestly thought we'd be all fogged in."

"Me, too. But what a nice surprise. I'm sure lunch will be delicious, too!" He no sooner raised his hand than a waiter materialized, reeling off the specials with the air of an out-of-work actor.

Anna began, "I have so many questions to ask I don't know where to start. It kind of came over me all in a rush this morning. That I really am here. That I'm coming back to stay."

"You know all this makes me happy?"

"I hope it does. It feels funny, somehow. Knowing that I'm taking over your job. Now it's real, I feel very uncertain and jumpy about it."

"Of course you do. It's a big step for one so young. But it's the right thing. I feel it. Here." He placed his hand on his heart and smiled at her. "Right for you. And right for the orchestra."

"But there's so much I need to learn. So much I need to know. Like how to be a good concertmaster, just for instance."

"You will learn quickly. You already play like someone much older and wiser. A remarkable sound for someone so young, so..."

"Female?" she suggested.

"Well, perhaps. Yours is an unusual gift, Anna. You hold nothing back, my child. I hear your soul in your music. Garrett heard it. He will help you learn, too."

The name jarred her. She didn't want it to, but she felt her pulse leap and her mind blur. She swallowed and pushed the feeling aside. "Tell me about the section, Simon. Tell me about the other violinists. Are they going to eat me alive?"

He looked relieved as the waiter brought their soup and gave him time to think. "It won't be easy, Anna. Musicians aren't saints, as you well know. They have their jealousies and spites. The man who will be your stand partner won't be pleasant, I'm afraid. He really wanted the job very much. But I think he'll come around."

"I think I'm more nervous than I was before."

"It won't be so bad." Simon steered the conversation to Anna's life back East and to music, and then talked about his own plans to visit relatives in Europe and Israel before returning to his Mercer Island home and settling into retirement.

They were nearly finished with the main course before she got up the nerve to ask about Garrett. "What do you think of him?"

Simon smiled at her unexpectedly. "Do you mean as a conductor or as a man?"

"Both, I guess."

"Well." Simon carefully cut a bite of his filet of sole and lifted it to his mouth. "I've known him a long time. As long as you, but differently, of course. I've watched him develop, watched him grow. He's a first-rate conductor, Anna. You must have sensed that yesterday. How much he's changed, evolved since you last played for him. Though it is hardly a fair test. You concentrate so hard, you forget to see. So intense an audition.

"I say this," he went on deliberately, "as someone who has worked with many great ones. I think by the time he is an old man like me he will be very famous. Though he will have to travel more than he does, perform before more audiences and probably move on to other orchestras. Of course, he's only been here a mere nine or ten years. That seems like a long time to people like you and Garrett. Ten years! It is nothing. The difference between seventy and eighty. What is that? No time in the life of a musician. Only in the life of a sports player!" He chuckled at his joke.

"And as a man?" she asked softly.

Simon thought over his answer for a long time. "As a man he is perhaps more difficult to understand. As a conductor he demands and commands and expects the best efforts of everyone in front of him and of himself, as well. And that's very good. As a man, he often does the same, which has won him perhaps few friends. However, he has been a good and true friend to me. We respect each other. Perhaps that is the key. Respect." He looked at her. "You will have to find your own key, Anna, with him. It will be essential for you to get along with him, to understand him. That will take time."

"What if we can't . . . work together well?"

He looked at her with a tilt of his head. "You think that will be a problem?"

"I don't know. I was just thinking."

"Don't think too much. Just play the music and let him do the thinking."

Anna laughed. "That sounds easy enough."

"Garrett's great love, after all, is the music. If one is lazy or stupid about something, he can be terrible. Unforgiving. But you are not lazy or stupid, so you have nothing to worry about, you see. He is very exciting to work with. I will miss that."

"I think you're still talking about the conductor," Anna reminded him gently. "How do you find him as a man? Trustworthy, for instance?"

"Yes. If I understand your meaning. He moves quickly and takes unexpected turns. Sometimes it feels like he's come up behind you just when you thought you saw him ahead down the road." Anna thought about the aptness of this description when she heard her companion say sadly, "I thought being married would settle Garrett a bit."

Her heart bumped against her throat. "He's married?" she blurted out.

"Not now, anymore. He was. Very happily, I thought. She was a soprano. Is, I should say. A lovely woman. Italian. Beautiful voice. She went to Chicago and I understand is doing very well there."

"When did they get married?" She tried to sound casual, tried not to find the subject as fascinating as she did.

"Let's see. About two, maybe three years ago. She's been gone since last summer. Since then, Garrett has, well, he's gotten even more intense, if that were possible."

"Do you know what happened?"

"Now, child, Garrett and I are close, but I don't know him that well. He is a very deeply private man. He doesn't give much of himself away. He hates to make mistakes, and since I'm sure he feels this marriage was a mistake, it is not something he would talk about to anyone."

He thought for a minute, stirring lemon into his tea. "You understand I've never tried to keep track of his personal life. He's always, shall we say, liked the ladies. But he never seemed keen on settling down. Then suddenly, it all happened rather quickly, he met this woman and he was a changed man. Very, very happy. Very much in love. Very much at peace, you know. And then everything went, well, kaput! I know it was very hard on him. For many weeks he was edgy and angry. Then he started really concentrating on the piano again, and he seemed to get back his, well, his balance, his sense of perspective.

"Did he tell you he's soloing in the *Emperor* at the end of the month?" He didn't wait for Anna's answer. "You know, I heard him play that twenty years ago in London. He was a mere boy. But for a boy, such power! Of course, he'd been performing all his life. If you can call what a child prodigy has a life. I remember watching him and thinking, he needs more time, more experience, he is like a robot, highly trained, but no depth."

Anna understood how Simon was steering the conversation and she realized she must follow. But she'd been struck by something. "This next concert, then, is his first piano concerto with the orchestra?"

"With any orchestra since his youth, as far as I know. He's worked hard this year, and has performed in small chamber groups all season. But I believe this is his first concerto in over twenty years. Shortly after I saw him that time in London, he just stopped performing. Walked away from it. Whether he had a breakdown or what, I don't know to this day."

"He sounded very confident when he mentioned the concerto last night. He acted like he did that sort of thing every day."

"He has a right to be confident. He's—well, extraordinary. If he can perform the way he rehearses, he should make a deep impression. The soul and heart he lacked at sixteen, he has now. Yes. But he's afraid. Privately, very afraid, I think."

"I'm always a little terrified before I perform."

"Anyone worth his salt is. But Garrett's nerves are very bad. His standards are extremely high, especially for his own work. The combination doesn't always work well."

"Are you the one who talked him into playing?"

"I think he convinced himself."

"Well, you talked me into playing my best at the audition. Don't underestimate your powers of persuasion."

"And now you're moving back to Seattle. Amazing."

"There's so much to do."

The rest of May dissolved as Anna found a place to live in Seattle, then flew back East to settle her affairs, pack up her belongings and arrange to have them shipped. On the very day of the gala concert she was wrestling boxes into a small rental house that perched halfway down the hill overlooking Lake Washington. A little gray-painted board-and-batten-style cottage with two tiny bedrooms, a living room and kitchen, it was the biggest space she'd lived in since her childhood. And it was near a bus route that would take her directly downtown to Seattle Center and the Concert Hall, as she confirmed that evening at seven o'clock.

Dead center in the first row of the first balcony, Anna sat alone amidst the crowd of the gala. Every seat was occupied. She read through the program and waited with everyone else. When the entire orchestra was seated and silent, Simon Weil walked slowly onto the stage with sure and measured steps. The house awarded him prolonged applause as he took his final bow as concertmaster, and he answered them with his customary smile. Anna watched him tune the orchestra and then take his seat. Now everyone waited.

She saw Garrett before the rest of the audience reacted. He really was astonishing, she thought reluctantly. She hadn't seen him since he'd dropped her off that night. She wasn't prepared for him now. Tall, fiercely dramatic under the lights, dressed regally in formal black and white, Garrett Downing swept onto the stage like a great black bird of prey as the applause from the capacity crowd rose deafeningly. As he bowed to the house, Anna applauded with the rest, quite convinced that everyone in Seattle adored this handsome, unpredictable maestro.

Abruptly he turned his back on them and stepped onto the podium. There was a moment of total, expectant silence, and then his baton came down swiftly to open the gala evening with the first insistent chords of Mozart's great *Jupiter* Symphony.

She'd already noticed that there was no music on the conductor's podium; all the complex sounds Garrett would conduct that evening were safely in his head. As the orchestra started the symphony's first themes, Anna sat forward in her chair, wishing she could see his face, wishing she were on stage playing for him.

Studying him, she knew that Simon had been right in predicting the younger man's future greatness. His precision was remarkable, his memory flawless, his command total and his enthusiasm contagious. The music seemed to come from his hands, spreading arcs of light and color through the rich sounds. She smiled to herself. She knew very well where the music came from. He was only a conductor, not a magician.

Before the final notes of the *Jupiter* died away, applause broke out and grew into a roar. Anna clapped and then laughed aloud, remembering suddenly the cheerful zeal of Seattle audiences. They loved to give standing ovations and did so generously.

Garrett's refreshingly daring interpretation of Mendelssohn's *Italian* Symphony reaffirmed Anna's growing conviction that her future boss was a genius.

During the intermission, she escaped the lobby's crush and smoke to wander in the gentle summer air and tried to still the race of her heart and reflect rationally on what she had just heard.

She had no one to talk to about her reactions. No one to share her feelings with. She had asked her Aunt Claire to come with her, but the woman declined, as Anna had known she would. Claire had a notoriously wooden ear, as she called it. She didn't enjoy music and refused to pretend to. So Anna was alone and bursting with excitement. She found a bench to sit on for a moment and let her mind wander backstage, trying to picture Garrett as he prepared himself to play the concerto. She thought about what Simon had said about Garrett's nerves and wondered how he was coping, how he was dealing with them. The lights in the lobby began to blink their warning.

The stage was ready: a magnificent ebony concert grand piano had been moved into position in the interim. The orchestra had returned and tuned up, and there he was again, covering the distance in long strides, bowing, then taking his place at the keyboard. His body was taut, ready.

There was a breathless hush. At a sign from Garrett, the orchestra sounded the first enormous chord of Beethoven's mighty *Emperor* Concerto. From the midst of that chord, his piano made its delicate entrance, a line of notes climbing upward and out of the torrent of sound, trilling and rippling alone for a moment before being covered by the next enormous chord. A magnificent beginning, breathed Anna to herself, as she unconsciously sat forward to drink it in.

Garrett had mastered the music and seemed in absolute control. He conducted with a natural ease from the keyboard, with nods of his head, glances, economical gestures. Again, it was evident to Anna that he had rehearsed his orchestra—and himself—rigorously, while somehow not losing any of the vitality, any of the sheer excitement of the great music. And the sounds he brought out of the instrument made Anna share Simon's joy in convincing him to perform again. He was brilliant.

As she had predicted, the enthusiastic audience rose as a body to give the concerto a standing ovation. Garrett made four trips back to the platform before he raised his hands to hush the commotion. Everyone rustled back into their seats and as the silence became general, he announced in a resonant baritone that easily reached the back rows that he was now going to put everyone in the mood for the party after the show. He took his seat once more at the keyboard and, smiling to himself, rolled out a Scott Joplin rag that brought a ripple of laughter through orchestra and audience alike. It was charming, Anna admitted, deftly played and just the right touch to launch the rest of the evening. This man knew exactly what he was doing.

In the rush and bumble of people rising and leaving the hall, Anna sat quietly, thinking over her next move. By rights, she should make her way backstage to speak to Simon and Garrett, and meet as many orchestra members as she could. Simon had invited her to do so, and she could not disappoint him. But she hesitated, dreading a false move or a wrong word at this point in a career that hadn't quite begun yet.

She needn't have worried. Simon was waiting for her, showing by his look that he knew what she was feeling. She rushed toward him with her arms outspread.

"It was fabulous, Simon!"

His eyes twinkled as he returned her embrace. "I thought we sounded pretty good tonight, if I say it myself. I'm so glad you were there. The seat was satisfactory?"

"You were the good fairy who arranged it. I should have guessed. It was perfect. I could see everything. And hear everything, of course."

"How did the piano sound?"

"Terrific. He was incredible, Simon. I've heard that thing a thousand times. But I feel like I just heard it for the first time."

"Go tell *him* that."

"Where is he?"

"Over there talking to the fellow who taped the concert. He'll get an advance copy and tear himself to pieces before twenty-four hours have passed. Then he'll start in on the orchestra."

"I dare him to find any major flaws." She looked around, but the man in question was striding toward a door in the wings to disappear as she watched.

Simon took her in hand and within minutes Anna had met several string players, a half dozen woodwinds, the timpanist and the principal French horn. Simon called out a name and a solidly built, balding man of around fifty turned and then scowled. Simon proceeded politely.

"Harold Corbett, this is Anna Terhune, whom you've heard about." Anna smiled and extended her hand. "Anna, this is Hal Corbett, your stand partner, the assistant concertmaster." Harold Corbett didn't want to shake her hand, she could tell. His mother must have brought him up well, however, because he finally did his duty and muttered "How do you do" between tense lips.

After he walked away Anna turned to Simon with wide eyes filled with mock terror and mouthed, "He's the one you told me about."

"Are you going to introduce me, Simon?" inquired an open-faced, thinnish young man with a black mustache, a mop of equally black hair and velvety brown eyes.

"Oh, yes, of course. Tom MacMahon, Anna Terhune. Tom's our principal cellist. You two will play in the orchestra quartet together. Tom came out from Baltimore two years ago."

"Part of the new wave from the East Coast," Tom declared, "finding refuge in the northwest."

"Well," Anna said easily, "I'm more like a prodigal daughter, back in the fold once more."

"How is it, coming back?" Tom wanted to know.

"So far it's all right. But I haven't done much except try to unpack a few boxes."

"That's not what I heard. Congratulations on your coup. News of your audition traveled fast. I only wish I'd been there to see it. I was doing a gig in San Francisco. Got to go for the money, sometimes," he added with a grin.

"Children, let's go to the party, shall we?" Simon interjected.

"I hope the food's good and there's plenty of it," Tom said. "I'm starved."

The young cellist tagged along with Simon and Anna. They reached the lobby to find a large buffet set up along one wall. The outer doors were open to reveal tables scattered throughout the courtyard. Across the way a low glass-walled building glowed with inner light, and through the open doors came the strains of a dance band swinging into the first set of the evening.

Suddenly Tom was asking Anna to dance and she found herself being led across the courtyard into the music. He danced choppily and chatted with her, discussing the concert, his own audition, his opinion of Seattle. Anna listened and, out of practice, concentrated on following his lead. She looked up to see Garrett through the crowd and stepped heavily on Tom's shiny toe.

A half hour passed before she saw Garrett again. She was seated alone on a bench, wondering whether to go in search of him to say the necessary words of congratulations when she saw him approaching. He was balancing a plate of edibles with a glass of champagne and he was alone. She shivered and for the first time wished she'd brought along a wrap of some sort. He hadn't seen her yet. When he did, she would rise, cross to him, extend her hand and... But how could she shake his hand when both were fully occupied? Well, she'd just get up and walk over and say—

Their eyes met and for an uncomfortable moment it was obvious to her that he wished he hadn't seen her. But he didn't look away. He just stood there, staring. What could she do but smile? He moved toward her then and she waited, wishing he would avert his gaze, not daring to avert her own.

When he stopped in front of her, his handsome face might have been a mask. "Ms. Terhune, our esteemed concertmaster-to-be, I presume."

Anna inclined her heard. "Maestro Downing, I believe." Games were easy.

"May I sit down?"

"Certainly." She moved a fraction of an inch to the right. He sat carefully so as not to crumple the tails of his jacket and put his champagne glass on the low wall behind them.

Her mind went completely, horribly blank. She watched him put away two pastry tidbits and sip some champagne. He smiled at her suddenly.

"So. How are things?"

"Fine," she replied automatically.

"All moved in?"

"More or less. Mostly less at this point," she added.

"You got Jennings's little house over in Madrona, didn't you?"

Her jaw dropped. "How did you know?"

"You gave my secretary your address and I recognized it. You're not the first musician to live there." He grinned. "Nice little house. Any problems?"

"No. Thanks."

He finished off the contents of the plate and swallowed the last of the champagne. She noticed that his hand seemed to be trembling slightly.

"Would you do me the honor of dancing with me?" he inquired with exquisite politeness. She could hear the band launching into something sweet and swingy. He raised his hand and nodded. "I know we agreed not to, well, interact socially, but I thought this once we could..."

"Of course," she said, unable to refuse. He rose and gave her his hand. As she stood up she could feel his eyes flickering down over her dress. It wasn't an extraordinary dress. Just one she'd bought for her master's recital two years ago. A deep rose silk, it had long tapered sleeves, a graceful neckline and a flattering drape to the waist and skirt.

When he led her to the floor and gathered her competently in his arms to begin the dance, her throat went abruptly dry and her breathing grew painfully shallow. She was enveloped in his presence and was aware only of his nearness, of the light pressure of his hand on the small of her back and of the texture of his other hand holding hers. As she followed his lead, trying to match his step, her heart drummed so wildly she was afraid her knees would give way. She stiffened and held herself carefully away from him. Only their clothing touched. It was like being in the midst of a whirlpool; she was being sucked steadily downward into some deep and unknown land.

Suddenly, his voice was there, softly next to her ear, "So what did you think of the concert?"

She blushed the color of her dress and looked up at him, missing a beat and stumbling over her words as she tried to make up for her oversight. "I'm sorry. Really, I've been looking for you since it was over to tell you how much I enjoyed it." He murmured a low thanks and she plunged on. "The orchestra sounded very good, I thought. The balance, the shading, everything. You really put new life into the music. And the concerto, Garrett, was excellent. It was like I'd never heard it before."

He accepted her praise without comment, but said after a moment, "So you don't have any second thoughts about . . ."

"Lord, no," she exclaimed. "I can't wait to get started. I kept wishing I was up there playing."

"Oh."

"I don't know. You seem to have thought everything out and knew exactly what you wanted."

He raised a quizzical eyebrow. "I believe that's the way it's done."

"Yes, no doubt, that's the intention. But in my experience, it doesn't always come out that way."

"In your experience," he echoed quietly, with a hint of a grin.

"But it did tonight," she went on enthusiastically, ignoring the irony in his voice. "I heard things as if they were new. I got all caught up in the music and forgot to listen critically. Honestly, I usually sit in a concert and spend the whole time picking apart all the violins and then start in on the rest. I can't help it. But tonight, it wasn't like that."

"Good. Anyway, that's *my* job."

"Simon warned me that you were still hypercritical."

"Simon should know."

They danced in silence for some minutes and Anna found herself torn between wishing the dance were over and wishing it would never end. He danced as if he were born to it, and he made her feel graceful and light. But his nearness had the effect of making her forget to breathe. She wanted to talk more about the music, especially the concerto. She had a thousand questions, but couldn't find the words she wanted.

"Did Simon tell you about the ticket he sent me?" she finally said. "The best seat in the house, besides his. I could see and hear everyone."

"Good. That was what I had in mind."

"You?"

"Simon, I mean." His face relaxed into a smile that reached his eyes. "We agreed you needed a good view. As to who actually set aside the tickets, it was Susan, my secretary, who made the arrangements and addressed the envelope. A conspiracy, you see."

He always seemed to be three steps ahead of her. "Thank you."

"You're quite welcome. You didn't use the other one?"

"No. My aunt doesn't enjoy concerts. I turned it in, and the man next to me seemed quite happy with it."

"Your aunt has never heard you play?"

"Not since I was about twelve."

He looked into her eyes then, so intently that she had to look away.

Abruptly, a figure in silver lamé collided with Anna's back and pushed her into her partner. He whirled gracefully away, holding her close. She fit against him as if she'd always belonged there. Her hair nestled against his jaw line, her cheek against his neck where it joined his shoulder. This was a new sensation for Anna, who'd never felt comfortable dancing. She closed her eyes and let herself relax against him. When the music ended she was thinking, it can't hurt, just this once.

They stood apart and she met his eyes. Eyes that were palest gray, wide-set and for that brief instant so full of regret and an unutterable yearning that Anna's throat closed up before she could protest.

"Did I pass?" he asked, a smile turning up one side of his long mouth.

"What?"

"No flirting, no innuendos... our agreement. Just wanted to make sure I did all right." His look had changed. His face might have been a mask, his eyes stones.

"Perfectly," she managed.

"Then I'll see you Wednesday night. Seven-thirty sharp. If you haven't already, pick up your music at the office. There's reams of it, and I want you to know it all yesterday."

He turned and left her.

Chapter Four

Garrett hadn't lied. There were piles of music scheduled for the Summer Festival, ranging from the sixteenth to the twentieth century, from orchestral works to duets. From mid-June through mid-August Anna saw she would be playing more music than she usually played in any given year. It was an exciting prospect, a real challenge, and one for which she found herself profoundly grateful. The schedule, with its endless array of rehearsals and performances, would leave no time for anything but music.

Not only was she acting as concertmaster for the five symphony concerts, Anna was also the first violinist in the Northwest Quartet, a string ensemble started by Simon Weil and composed of Northwest Symphony members. Their first performance was to be the last Saturday night in June when the four string players would perform an evening of piano quintets with Garrett at the piano. Anna was also scheduled to play in an assortment of other groups, as well as a series of six Sunday afternoon recitals for violin and piano. With Garrett at the keyboard.

Garrett. He was unavoidable yet to be avoided. Even though he was everywhere in her day, he could be nowhere in her mind and heart. As the days of the first week passed, Anna was relieved to see that he was going to make it easy for her. He seemed to have forgotten she existed. He seemed to have forgotten that she was his concertmaster. He only spoke to her when it was mandatory. He was firmly in his own world, taciturn, self-confident and unassailable.

As a conductor, from the very first orchestra rehearsal, Garrett Downing was a revelation to Anna. Simon hadn't exaggerated; the man was amazing. He attacked each work with rigor. He took nothing for granted, but went over passages endlessly, challenging, correcting, bringing everyone in the orchestra to an understanding of his vision of the music, a vision firmly based on thorough research combined with an uncanny instinct. He worked his musicians hard, but he worked himself harder. Words of praise didn't seem to belong in his vocabulary, Anna noted ruefully, but he had no trouble expressing himself eloquently when finding fault. No one escaped his scathing criticism, including Anna.

It was only the second rehearsal when she found herself suddenly on the hot seat. The orchestra was scheduled to open the festival with two consecutive evenings featuring all six of Bach's *Brandenburg* Concertos. While Garrett had distributed the many solos among various orchestra members, he had relegated to Anna the plummy solos in the First and Fourth Concertos.

In the middle of the rapid first movement of the Fourth, Garrett brought the group to an abrupt halt and impaled Anna with a pale gray stare. "This is not a practice session for your benefit," he told her.

She widened her eyes and lifted her chin. "I know that," she replied in a voice she wished was firmer.

"I'm hearing tentative playing. Vagueness. As if you weren't quite sure what you were doing here. Do you know what you're doing here?" But before she could find the words she needed to answer him, he'd turned to the woodwind section and was skewering all of them for "muddiness." Then he fell silent while the orchestra members adjusted themselves in their seats. "Let's try it from the top. You know what this is supposed to sound like. Play it that way. Do your practicing on your own time." This last he directed at Anna before tapping his baton and making any reply impossible.

She could only respond by playing the music. By concentrating on the notes and the sound. By driving every other thought out of her head. She had to put the rest of her life on hold. Her ugly purple-and-green bathroom. Her lawn that needed mowing. Grocery shopping. The wicker sofa the man said he'd deliver some afternoon that week, but couldn't say when. The car she didn't own, didn't want to own, didn't have time to find but would probably have to get somehow since the city buses were driving her crazy. The kiss she'd shared with a man who now wouldn't give her the time of day. The man himself. The man she couldn't think about yet had to face nearly every hour of every day.

The afternoon after he criticized her Bach, she faced her first rehearsal alone with him, to work on the violin/piano sonatas. She told herself once it was over she'd be all right. She told herself that the first time would be the worst, and after that she'd know what was expected of her. All the way down the hall, she tried to think only of the music, not the man on the other side of the door who was waiting for her and her alone.

The rehearsal room door loomed up in front of her. She stared at it for a long time, her stomach in a knot, her throat tight with tension. Her neck and shoulders ached from long hours of playing and practicing. She dreaded opening the door and finding him at the piano, glaring at her. She put her hand on the knob and opened it slowly.

The room was empty and her breath came out in a rush. The shiny grand piano stood idly in the center of the room. Several chairs and music stands were scattered about. Foam cups that might have once been filled with coffee sat forgotten on a table. Anna moved them aside, put her violin case down and opened it. It was then she realized she was shaking. Trembling all over. She drew a big breath and told herself aloud, "This is ridiculous!"

"What's ridiculous?" came a voice behind her.

She whirled and found Garrett standing in the doorway. His head was tilted to the side. He looked almost relaxed, in pleated tan slacks and an open-necked striped shirt, holding a file full of music low on his hip. His nose showed signs of recent sunburn. She said, "Nothing. I talk to myself."

"I'll remember that," he said and shut the door behind him.

Anna wasn't sure she'd be able to breathe. The room seemed suddenly small and he seemed to fill it completely. She stood stock still while he seated himself at the keyboard and set out his music. After a moment he looked over at her. "Don't you think you'd better get your violin out?"

She nodded but couldn't move. She felt hopelessly foolish. She wanted to run. She tried to form words.

"What's the matter?" No concern in his voice. Just a kind of studied indifference. Almost annoyance.

"I don't think I can play," she stammered, and wished she were dead.

"Why on earth not?"

She closed her eyes and before she could think of an alternative, she blurted out the truth. "I'm shaking too much. I'm sorry."

"What's wrong?"

"I don't know." This was a lie, but she couldn't tell him the truth. "Nerves, I guess."

"This isn't exactly a performance, you know."

"I'm sorry. I don't know what to do about it."

"Just start in and play. It'll go away."

"Not before you've sliced me to ribbons," she muttered under her breath.

"What?"

Anna looked away, regretting her words. Now she'd have to admit that he terrified her. It was degrading. It wasn't even entirely true. But she didn't know how else to explain her trembling. She turned her back on him and began to close up her violin case. "I just don't think I can play duets with you."

"Turn around." When she faced him he was still sitting at the piano. "This isn't a voluntary organization. You and I are playing the sonatas, and that's an end to it. Whether you don't want to or don't feel up to it or whatever, really has nothing to do with it. It's your job."

"There are other violinists. . . ." she countered.

"Yes. But you're my concertmaster and that's part of the deal, you see. We're going to play for people who might not bother to come to the symphony concerts. We're going to show them what they're missing. So for me to perform with somebody who sits in the back of the violin section just doesn't quite do the job. Do you understand?"

Anna swallowed and nodded.

"Haven't you practiced?"

"Of course I've practiced," she replied through clenched teeth.

"Then I fail to see the problem. We're wasting time here. Time we really don't have to waste. So get that fiddle out and tune it up and let's get on with it. We'll start with the Brahms. That went pretty well at your audition."

The first fifteen minutes were sheer hell for Anna. She knew the music as well as her own name. She knew what she wanted it to sound like. But her fingers seemed to have minds of their own. At every moment she expected Garrett to stop the music and lace into her. She could sense his impatience, his intolerance, his disgust. But he didn't stop, and he didn't say a word. He played his part fluently, delicately filling in around and behind her instrument, and she gradually found herself relaxing into the job. The man disappeared from her thoughts, and the glorious sound of the piano replaced him. Her violin began to speak to that alone, and then there was only music.

"That wasn't so bad," he said quietly in the silence after they finished the last movement. "Needs work, but it'll come. You seem to have recovered."

She nodded, wondering how they could be so compatible musically and barely able to communicate the rest of the time. No hellos for them, no niceties; they couldn't even use each other's names. But their music was in a different dimension. She knew she wouldn't be afraid of it again.

"Let's try that first movement once more," he was saying, "and then go on and take a good look at the Franck sonata."

The Northwest Quartet quickly became the sole joy of Anna's life. No Garrett to deal with during these rehearsals. She looked forward to them as she did to dreamless sleep. Tom MacMahon, the velvet-eyed cellist from Baltimore, held up the lower end of the quartet. Charlotte and Clark Phillips, a married couple in their mid-thirties, played viola and second violin respectively. Charlotte, a tall, strongly built woman with alarmingly red hair, was a down-to-earth person who had a predilection for health food and gossip. Her husband, Clark, blond, bespectacled and prematurely bald, was one of the most relaxed people Anna had ever met.

By definition the four musicians were the top string players in the orchestra, each the head of their particular section, and as the rehearsals progressed, Anna felt her confidence grow. She'd played with many other quartets, but she'd never experienced the solidarity she felt with this group. Together they survived surprise visits from Garrett, who dropped randomly by to "listen in for a bit" and left them with pithily worded nuggets of criticism.

One day during a quick lunch at the Food Circus at Seattle Center, Anna learned a number of things from Charlotte that explained Garrett's behavior as a music director. "When I first came," the older woman told her, "five years ago this fall, he had a different style. We were kind of like a big happy family. But over the past couple years he's changed. I'm not sure, you know, that it hasn't been for the best, as far as the orchestra is concerned. But he's cut himself off from us. He's not a friend anymore. Not, you know, somebody you'd want to have to dinner on a free night. It's like he has to keep his distance. It's tightened up the group, and while people grumble a lot about him, I doubt if there's a single one of us who'd quit. He's too good."

"Does he ever say anything good about anyone's work?"

"Praise, you mean?" Charlotte had to think. "Well, his best praise is a kind of quiet smile. It means he's not going to criticize you. If you play it the way he wants you to, the way he hears it in that incredible head of his, then he just kind of smiles as if to say, 'Well, I knew it was there all along. Glad you finally made it.'"

"I find I really dread rehearsals with him," Anna admitted.

"He's been particularly awful lately, you're right. Honestly I think he's just uptight about the Festival. It's his baby, you know. He pushed it through and got it funded, but I've heard—and this is strictly confidential—that his job is on the line. If he can't pull in the numbers, he's out. And if that's the case, the orchestra is in big trouble. They've laid off two dozen musicians in the last year. There are all kinds of rumors. But everyone is proceeding as if everything's perfectly fine. I guess you have to. But Garrett's got to be worried."

The next day was Saturday and Anna had the whole, entire afternoon to herself, her first since rehearsals began. She hauled an ancient push mower, which seemed to belong to the house, out of her basement and mowed her tiny lawn. She planted the box of pansies she found at a corner market and brought home on the bus. And as she worked, she thought. She thought about what Charlotte had said, and she thought about Garrett's situation. If his attitude was really a case of nerves, then maybe she should say something to him. He needed friends not enemies. They were all together in this thing. But how could she say anything? The only time she saw him alone was when they were working on the sonatas. He wasted no time in idle chatter. He came, they worked, he left. And during the piano quintet rehearsals, when one would think he would relax a bit, he was tighter than ever, merciless, relentless, demanding.

She dug in the dirt with jabbing motions of the spoon she'd found to do service as a trowel, then pressed the moist earth around the last of the cheerful little pansies. The afternoon sun was warm on her back. It reminded her how sore her muscles were. It also reminded her it was time to practice. She had a rehearsal this evening and another tomorrow. She stood up, dusting her hands off on her jeans. Out of the corner of her eye she caught a glimpse of movement.

A lone jogger was pumping steadily up the hill, his head tucked down. Lean and brown, his long legs glistening and sinewy, his brown hair tangled in a red sweatband, he held white hand weights and the muscles and veins stood out in relief on his arms. Dressed in navy shorts and a sweat-stained gray T-shirt, he ran with an easy grace. He climbed the street steadily, his neck muscles straining, his face drenched despite the sweatband.

As he came to the corner opposite her house he lifted his head and Anna recognized the runner. Garrett. Her lips parted as she gasped then caught herself. He made a left turn and rounded the corner by her house without slowing his pace. She stood motionless, praying silently that he wouldn't see her. But as he passed by, perhaps ten yards away, he glanced her way over the low picket fence. Time balanced precariously for an instant, and stopped completely as Garrett hesitated, halted after another stride and finally stood, hands at his sides, staring at her from the opposite side of the quiet street. A bird screeched and rose in a black whorl from the top of the monkey tree across the street.

Anna stared back. She watched him lift his shirt and use its tail to wipe his face, and her mouth went dry. The movement revealed a taut waist, a glimpse of body hair. Her breath caught in her throat. He was beautifully put together, his thinness a deception, for his limbs were strong, his shoulders broad, his body perfectly conditioned. He looked like an athlete not a musician.

"Settled in?" His voice carried easily over the distance.

"Almost."

"You've got a view."

"Yes." She remembered with a jolt that not two minutes before she'd wanted to talk to him. And here he was. She couldn't remember what it was she wanted to say.

They stood in silence for another moment then he bent over abruptly to massage a calf muscle. He looked up at her. "Cramp," he said. "Have to keep moving. I shouldn't have stopped. See you." She watched him shake his leg out, gather himself up and head off, gathering speed until he rounded the corner and disappeared.

Neither of them mentioned the meeting during the days that followed. It seemed to Anna that they'd developed a kind of shorthand speech that communicated so little as to be nearly nonexistent. He didn't really speak to her at all, she realized, except to complain about her playing or suggest a new approach or correct a 'misconception' or push a tempo to the breaking point. But now Anna could see that his treatment of her wasn't unique. He was always alone, arriving and leaving all the rehearsals by himself, only speaking when he had something critical to say. She found herself remembering how Simon had counseled her to learn to get along with him, to respect him, to try to understand him. She wished she could talk to

Simon now and ask his advice in dealing with Garrett, but he was across the ocean in another world.

There was nothing she could do, she told herself, except her job. That's all Garrett was asking of her.

But one morning that became impossible. The morning the nine-fifteen bus didn't ever come. By quarter to ten, standing in the shelter out of the rain, Anna knew she was in trouble. It took another twenty minutes to find a cab. She told the driver to hurry and then wished she hadn't for she couldn't open her eyes once during the ride. She was too scared even to rehearse her excuses.

As she went down the corridor, still trembling from the horrible taxi ride, she realized that the orchestra was well into the Fourth *Brandenburg* Concerto and someone else was playing her part. She went through a side door into the auditorium and stood in the aisle to watch. Sure enough, Hal Corbett, her stand partner and cross to bear, was playing the violin solo. All Garrett would have had to have done was change the order of the rehearsal. But no, that would have been too simple. She came on stage between movements.

Garrett stared at her. "Did we disturb your beauty sleep?"

She ignored the implication and went for straight confession. "I'm sorry I am late. My bus never showed up and taxis are hard to come by, it turns out. And when you find one, you're lucky to reach your destination alive."

"You mean to tell me you depend on public transportation to get around?"

"I didn't know it was a crime."

"It is if it makes you late for a rehearsal. Now, thank Hal for being on time and taking your place for the second movement. We've wasted enough time. In case it's slipped your mind, we're performing these things next week. For an audience. And we're not ready yet." These last words he addressed to the orchestra at large.

Her thank-you died on her lips under the scathing look Corbett gave her. Theirs was an uneasy relationship at best, and this would take weeks to undo. Swallowing her anger she unpacked her instrument, attacked the movement cold and was not happy with her sound. Neither was Garrett. Nevertheless, Anna survived his sarcasm and finished the rehearsal feeling as if she'd done a decent job under the circumstances.

That same afternoon Anna faced another rehearsal with Garrett and the quartet. If only, she thought, it were just the quartet. That would have been fine. But they were performing the piano quintets at the end of the month, and Garrett had squeezed in an extra rehearsal. It was rigorous, wonderful music, but with Garrett there, always there, stopping and starting and trying for new effects, challenging, harping, complaining, demanding, it was anything but enjoyable. As first violin, Anna led the quartet, and her leadership was acknowledged as right, unquestioned, accepted by the other three. Her leadership should have carried over to the quintet, but Garrett didn't allow it.

"Anna." She started at his use of her name and looked at him. One eyebrow had lifted high on his forehead and his eyes glittered with annoyance. "Would you mind concentrating a little? Everyone else is playing in key. You seem to have invented a new one."

The remark brought a variety of nervous snorts from the other three musicians, and Anna felt herself glow red hot with embarrassment. "I'm sorry," she muttered. "I was thinking about the last passage."

"You have a problem with the last passage?"

She bit her lip and said in a low voice, "I don't agree with your approach to it."

"I beg your pardon?"

"I said I don't agree..."

"I heard that. Do you want to elaborate?" He had crossed his long legs and grabbed his knee with both hands. His head was cocked at her and she couldn't meet his hard eyes.

Anna felt her heart quaver within her chest. She'd tried to argue with him before. It hadn't ever gone well. She clenched her jaw and began, "I think..."

"Yes?"

She closed her eyes tightly for an instant and tried to forget to whom she was speaking. She said the words carefully. "I think that we should slow down a bit there as the phrase ends. It's not exactly indicated, but it would be effective, I think. It seems to me you're...we're rushing it and ruining the mood." Her voice ran down.

"Are you finished?"

"Yes."

"Thank you for your opinion." He turned his body back to the keyboard and scanned the music. "Anyone else care to contribute?" The silence was general. Tom cleared his throat and shifted in his chair, shooting a furtive, clearly apologetic glance to Anna. "All right, let's begin again at the double bar. And remember, gently here and with great emotion. But don't glom it on. And don't cover me up. And, Charlotte, let that viola sing out."

Anna played with all her heart, trying to forget herself and her humiliation by concentrating on the music. After all, it wasn't the first time he had put her down. It wouldn't be the last. It doesn't matter, she told herself. But her concentration faltered, a small error led to more mistakes, and Anna grew more and more rattled. Garrett had something cutting to say to her every time they paused, and her depression began to change back to anger. Finally, with a glance at his watch and a mild curse, Garrett called a halt. Anna packed up quickly and left the room.

She found an empty practice room, put her violin case down and paced the small area angrily. She sat down at the piano and pounded out some raucous chords. Enough was enough, she told herself. She couldn't work with him anymore. She'd go tell him so. She'd quit. She'd hit him right on his beautiful nose. She didn't understand why the entire orchestra didn't rise in mutiny against him. She didn't understand any of it.

Anna knew that if she let her anger die, her momentum would fall away with it, so she straightened her shoulders, grabbed her instrument, flung back her hair and marched up to his office. Garrett's secretary, a woman for whom Anna felt at that moment a profound mixture of pity and respect, looked up from her typewriter and smiled. Anna managed to smile back and ask in a controlled voice if Mr. Downing was in. The woman nodded and buzzed the intercom. She told him Anna was there and apparently he consented to see her.

Anna looked at the door and wished her heart would quit pounding and her legs weren't trembling. She gritted her teeth, walked over and knocked too loudly.

"Come in."

She did as he instructed then closed the door with her back to it, gathering strength from the firmness behind her.

He wasn't looking at her. He'd changed into a three-piece pale linen suit and looked devastating. He was gathering papers into an ordinary briefcase. "I'm rather pressed for time," was all he said.

"I have to talk to you."

At least he looked at her then. For what seemed like an hour. Then he glanced away and seemed to be considering her request. "All right," he said at last. "Sit down. But I really don't have much time."

Anna came in and perched on the edge of the upholstered chair. It was a beautiful office, furnished with teak and leather and carpeted in textured earth tones. The windows behind the large cluttered desk yawned widely over the main courtyard of Seattle Center.

Garrett waited, his face an impassive challenge.

Everything she'd wanted to say raged through her head. And dissolved into, "I don't understand. What on earth is going on?"

"I beg your pardon?" He wasn't going to give an inch.

"Don't do this, please. Don't act like we're total strangers. Just talk to me."

There was a brief silence. Then he sat down carefully behind his desk and rested his head against his upraised hands for an instant. When he looked at her again, his expression was unreadable. "I have nothing to say."

"Well. I guess I do." She stood up and sat down again. "You hired me to be your concertmaster. But you haven't once treated me like one. You act as if you're alone against the whole world and that the members of your orchestra are your worst enemies. You can't do anything but criticize and then wonder when we get a little shaky from time to time.

"The orchestra," she repeated, then drew a breath as she gathered her thoughts. "I can't argue with what you're doing, really. You'd always have the last word anyway. And I think your ideas are great, mostly. It's the execution that stinks."

"Are you finished?" He had stood up.

Anna stood also. "No. No, I'm not. I've listened to you for the last couple of weeks. Now you can listen to me for a minute. Because I can't work like this. Your approach to chamber music makes me sick. I mean, in chamber music, all the members of the group have to be able to communicate with each other on equal footing. They have to be able to criticize each other without personal feelings being involved. It's a give and take thing, you know? The rest of the quartet and I get along fine, wonderfully, but when you're there, I can't make a peep without feeling like an idiot. So I'm asking you to back off. Please. Now I've finished." And perhaps, she thought as she sat down, she really was. Her heart was beating so fast she could barely breathe.

Remarkably, he didn't say a word. He walked away from his desk over to the window, then turned to face her. She met his eyes, then couldn't look away. His voice was low. "Get out of here," he said.

"Are you firing me?"

"Right now I wish I could."

"Garrett." She said his name and stopped. His gaze would not leave her. Tension filled the room and Anna knew she'd either have to speak now or leave forever. "I didn't really come here wanting to fight. Oh, maybe I did. But I was really upset over what happened with the Schumann quintet just now. I don't like being rattled so much I lose control. And this morning—when I was late—it wasn't really my fault. And you could have started the rehearsal with another piece. You didn't have to do that to me. I've thought all along it was me, you know. I've felt you were singling me out, trying to test me or something, or to punish me for...well. Whatever. But I've gradually realized that you're out to get us all. What I don't understand is why. You need us, you know. You can't do the whole festival by yourself. You've got to convince us you believe we can pull it off, not convince us you think we're all incompetent fools." She stopped and drew a noisy breath. "But I'm not here to tell you how to do your job."

"That's odd." One side of his mouth lifted. "I thought that was exactly what you were doing."

She tried to chuckle. "I guess I am. I'm sorry."

He blew out a slow breath and she saw a ghost of a smile float across his face. "No, you're not. You may even be right about some things. Not about everything."

Slowly he returned to his chair, propped his elbows on his desk and studied her before he continued. "My criticism isn't meant to be personal in any way. If I seemed to concentrate on you a bit more than anyone else, it's because I need to know how much you can give me. Your technical range in the Bach, for instance. Your emotional range in all that Romantic stuff we're doing together. I'll let up when I hear what I want. If you want me to say I'm beginning to hear it, then fine. Consider it said."

She listened to his words, recognized them as the faintest of praise and found herself noticing details of his face. The spring of his nostril, the shape of his strong chin, the small cleft that gave it character, the hollows beneath his high cheekbones, the tiny lines at his eyes, the deeper lines around his mouth, the shape of his mouth.

"As far as orchestra rehearsals are concerned," he was saying, "I never change the order. It's a quirk of mine. Changing things around to suit a whim is unprofessional, I feel. You may disagree with that. But I'd advise you never to be late again." He didn't wait for her response. "As for the rest of your complaints, I'm not sure how to answer them or even if I have to. It sounds as if you're accusing me of acting like a conductor. Which is a lot different from being a teacher or a baby-sitter. Perhaps at school that's what you got used to. But out here in the real world, you people have a job to do, and it's my job to see you do it.

"Which brings us to what happened just now with the Schumann. You may not realize how much time

I've put in on these quintets, on top of everything else I've taken on..."

"We've all put time in on them," she interjected. "Every one of us."

His lips tightened to a line. "Granted," he said. "But if you're going to fall apart anytime somebody disagrees with one of your half-baked ideas about..."

She stood up. "Not anybody. Just you. Because of how you do it. You see, I respect you, Garrett. I take you seriously. I guess you don't respect me or think me good enough to take seriously. I'd thought a lot about that particular passage and you wouldn't even listen to me."

"I listened. I disagreed. And you fell apart. Can you explain that? Frankly," he added, "I was astonished."

She couldn't answer him. She knew if she didn't get out of there she would start crying, and she'd rather die then have him see that. She made a show out of looking at her watch. "Oh, I've made you late for something. I didn't mean to be here this long." She turned away and cursed a tear that dropped on her hand. She wiped it away, praying he hadn't seen it.

"I have a few more minutes," he told her when she'd reached the door, her back to him. "And I really think we ought to finish what you've started here."

Anna turned to face him, knowing and hating that her cheeks were wet. "Why in heaven's name did you hire me?" she asked him hoarsely.

He took a long time to think over his answer. "You had a sound I wanted, Anna Terhune. I haven't heard it often since. Only when we play. You and I. So I know it's there. I hope to God I hear it next week when we perform the Bach."

She looked away and sniffed.

"Are you crying?" he asked incredulously.

"No," she lied, and then the dam broke. "I'm tired and a little discouraged right now. A lot discouraged. I'd hoped we could talk. Not snipe at each other. I feel like I'm working in a vacuum with you, Garrett. And I guess I'm finding out I can't work like that. Like this, I mean. I'm not asking for much. Just friendship. God, that sounds crazy. I'd hoped... well, it's silly, really. I'd hoped maybe I could convince you I was on your side. But you don't seem to want anybody on your side. I know you might be thinking about what happened between us that night. I know I think about it. And about the dance we had. And about what we decided to do about all that. Nothing, I mean. Maybe it doesn't have anything to do with what's been happening. But somehow I feel it does. And if it doesn't, then—" She knew she was babbling. His voice stopped her, and his touch. A voice she hadn't heard in ages, a touch she'd tried to forget.

"Anna," he said. He'd moved slowly as she'd spoken with her gaze anywhere but on him, and now there was no distance between them, and he put out his hand and spoke her name. Very gently he lifted the hair from her cheek and pushed it back. She had to pull away from him. He frowned and dropped his hand to his side.

"I'm not very good at friendship," he said. "I've tried to keep my distance from you, to make it easier to put aside what I feel. Perhaps that's affected my behavior toward you. I don't think so. I've made an effort to treat you the same way I treat everyone. An effort, Anna. It hasn't been easy. Only necessary. You'd made it quite clear you had no interest in me as a man. I don't hold that against you. You've probably shown great good sense. But I guess I forgot that there might be a middle ground." He smiled. "Like friendship. What an idea."

He produced a large white handkerchief, waited until she took it and walked to his desk and half sat against it.

"I'm not going to change my style," he declared. "While I suppose I admire the courage it took for you to come here, I'm not going to alter my conducting methods. The rest of the orchestra knows me better than you. They understand what I'm doing. You'll understand better after next week." He sighed. "About the quintets, I admit I've been a bit of a tyrant. I'll try to curb my impulses at the next rehearsal. We'll play it your way and see how it goes. Fair enough?"

Chapter Five

Anna would have given her soul to relive the day. She'd looked forward to this one free evening in her week, and now it was all in tatters. She'd made a complete and utter fool of herself. That at the end Garrett had softened a little and conceded one point didn't help when she remembered that it had been her tears which had softened him. Tears! She closed her eyes and groaned aloud.

She didn't even remember how she'd gotten home. The usual bus ride, she knew. But she didn't remember a single yard of it, she was so involved in examining and reexamining every moment of that dreadful day. Now she was home, standing in her little kitchen, realizing she should eat something, but at a loss to know what. She opened her refrigerator, hoping something would leap out at her.

A rusty head of iceberg lettuce, a carton of outdated plain yogurt, a bag of cherries, probably moldy, two only slightly prunish tomatoes. The freezer held a half-empty carton of chocolate-chip ice milk, a frozen chicken filet entrée and a package of frozen lasagna. With a sigh Anna popped the lasagna into the oven and set about trying to ferret out edible lettuce fragments. She was going to have to go to a grocery store soon or starve to death.

Water running over the lettuce brought back the memory of the morning's rain, and then she was thinking about crying again. If only she'd swallowed her anger and never gone to his office. What had she hoped to accomplish? She couldn't believe she'd pleaded for friendship. For she wasn't at all sure she could handle being friends with somebody like Garrett. He'd kissed her, he'd danced with her, and both times, before she'd had a chance to realize what a mistake it all was, she'd responded blindly. But both times, she had succeeded in pushing back, in putting him off completely. And now she'd acted impulsively and thrust herself right back into the ring.

Maybe not, she thought. He hadn't really said anything much. He'd barely touched her. Just pushed her hair back. Her damned hair that never was in the right place. And offering her a handkerchief was hardly a sign of . . . love.

She picked at the lettuce and muttered to herself. "It's not love we're talking about here. It's desire. Lust. Physical attraction."

That was the key. For it would have been so simple if . . . if Garrett didn't look the way he looked. Physical attraction was just something that happened, she assured herself as she hunted for the ingredients for salad dressing. It wasn't something a person could help. But it was something she'd dealt with before. It didn't have to get in the way. A crush. She smiled at the thought. She'd had crushes. She'd even had a crush on Garrett before. When she was seventeen and he a mystifying, maddening, remote man of twenty-nine. Now he was thirty-seven or eight and she was old enough to know better than to let somebody's handsome face and well-made body make her heart speed up. It was unthinkable. She was getting it all confused again. If only she hadn't let herself cry.

She wrenched her mind away from him and thought about her music. She ate her dinner at her new table and watched the light gradually fade from the day. Full darkness was still hours away. Sunsets came late in June in the Northwest. She let herself wonder whether Garrett was looking out some window and noticing the way the high clouds were shot with pink, the way the mountains were etched in black against the pale sky, the way the water reflected the pink and the black. She closed her eyes. Better to imagine him snoozing in his chair with his mouth open, snoring noisily, unattractive, human.

The shrill ring of the phone broke in on her fantasies and made her realize how silent the house was. She checked her watch. Just after nine Thursday night. This time next week they'd be just starting the second half of their first concert. Lord.

"Hello?"

"Anna." Her name was enough.

"Yes."

"This is Garrett."

"I know." Her lips formed the syllables, but no sound came out.

"Are you there?"

"Are you calling to fire me?"

She heard, incredibly, the sound of laughter. "No. Not this time. But don't push me. Listen. I've been thinking about what you said." He sighed.

She rushed in. "I was very upset. I said a lot I shouldn't have. Sometimes I should just count to ten and forget it."

"Perhaps. But what if I said you were right about a few things. I've been strung pretty tight lately. The fact is, losing Simon was kind of a blow. I didn't expect to miss him so much. I hadn't really realized how much I depended on him. He was my go-between, you know, between me and the orchestra. And I haven't given you the chance to be that. I wasn't sure how to go about it, after what happened."

Anna found she was holding the receiver very tightly. Slowly she slipped down to a sitting position on the floor.

"There's a lot at stake this summer. More than I want to think about. I don't know what you've heard. Hell, the board tells me something new every week. But I've been working hard to keep everything afloat the last few months. And I've been more difficult than I should have been." He stopped. "Why is this easier over the phone?"

"Maybe because I'm keeping my mouth shut."

He laughed again, softly. "Anyway, I can't promise any radical change in my behavior. But it occurred to me that one way of, well, getting the quintet more together was to admit that I was the problem."

"I didn't say that."

"Not exactly. But I think it's an accurate assessment. I've heard the four of you, and you do have an uncanny ability to communicate. And I know you and I have the potential of playing very well together. If I'm not happy with the quintets, maybe—notice the maybe, please—the problem lies with me. So I was thinking that perhaps if we changed something—if, for instance, the four of you came to my house tomorrow for the rehearsal. It would be less formal. I like my own piano much more than that damned beast in the rehearsal room...."

"It sounds like a good idea."

"Not to mention that I've just been informed that Seattle Center will be crawling with small ballet dancers tomorrow giving their annual recital."

It was Anna's turn to laugh.

"Do you think you could come? I've already called the others, and it's fine with them. Though they might well be in shock," he added with a chuckle.

"It sounds great. Of course I'll come." She swallowed. Her mouth was terribly dry. "But I don't know where you live."

"I'm not sure of the bus route, but I'm not too far from your aunt's house. I think you were here once a thousand years ago with Simon. I'm over on the Lake Union side of Capitol Hill just west of Volunteer Park." He named the address, and Anna remembered the house clearly, just as if a slide had clicked into place on a screen.

"I can get there easily."

"I could give you a ride."

"That won't be necessary. But thanks."

There was another silence. "I was wondering." He cleared his throat. "Did you happen to notice the evening. The light is extraordinary. It must be beautiful from your window."

"The tops of the Cascades are still catching the light, but the lake is amazing." She couldn't get her voice to sound normal. There seemed to be no air in her lungs.

"The sun just disappeared behind the Olympics. There's a line of clouds to the southwest, the most incredible shades of violet."

Anna closed her eyes and, before she could capture the words, they leaked out. "What did you have for supper?"

She couldn't believe she'd asked him. She couldn't believe that he didn't seem to think her question the least bit odd. "Well, let's see. A rather nice veal chop braised in fresh vegetables. Saffron rice. A bit of melon. And a, shall we say, subtle but pleasant St. Michelle Chardonnay."

"You cooked all that?"

He chuckled. "Yes. Except for the wine. It's not so very hard. Especially if you like to eat. You don't look as if you like to eat."

"Thanks a lot."

"I just mean you look like the yogurt-and-salad type."

"Well, I had lasagna tonight, thank you."

"Good?"

"Awful." She sighed. "It was frozen."

"Oh."

"I hate to cook."

"I see."

She bristled at his tone. "Not all of us are as talented as you."

There was a brief pause before he asked pleasantly, "I thought we'd called a truce, Anna. You sound as if you're trying to pick a fight."

"No. Just stating a fact. I guess I'm defensive about my cooking. Or, rather, my not cooking."

As they both drew a breath, an absurd hope nudged Anna's brain. Maybe he would ask her over or invite himself over. She wanted to see him. Suddenly, irrationally, it was important to see him. To be with him. To talk to him. To find out everything about him.

"Well," he said, "I'll see you tomorrow then at about half past two. All right?"

"Yes," she answered. "All right."

Garrett threw open the door of his house, and she could hear the other string players tuning up inside. He was freshly showered and shaved, dressed in a vivid aqua polo shirt and white cotton pleated slacks. She took in the faint limy tang of his after-shave, the dampness of his hair where it curled at his neck, and couldn't keep back a smile. "Sorry I'm a minute late."

His eyebrows arched over clear gray eyes. "Bus trouble?"

"No." Up went her chin. "I dawdled. It's such a gorgeous day."

First, she'd taken a long time deciding what to wear and opted for the simplest of skirts, a cotton Indian print, and a cotton gauze blouse. The day was bright and hot, and by the time she'd walked the blocks from the bus to Garrett's house, she was glad of her choice. And then, the walk itself had taken longer than she'd planned because it had all been so beautiful. Garrett's section of Capitol Hill was more secluded than Claire's, a few blocks distant from Volunteer Park, and one of the oldest neighborhoods in Seattle, full of gracious homes, enormous trees, dense greenery lush from the summer rains. Flowers whose names Anna couldn't remember filled the sunny air with heavy perfume. Long graceful ferns nodded as she passed.

She'd turned the last corner and seen Garrett's house hidden in an elbow of a street that turned abruptly east. With the air of a misplaced farmhouse, it perched with turn-of-the-century primness on the hill that dropped off to the freeway far below and Lake Union beyond that. A walk curved off the driveway and led through a gate in the chest-high slatted fence.

"Well, you're forgiven for dawdling," Garrett said as he stepped aside to let her in. "This once. Come in so we can get started and get finished before the day is gone completely."

Garrett's living room was mostly piano, a black, satin-finish grand that stretched itself before an L of windows. His furniture was comfortable-looking, casually elegant, oak trimmed, overstuffed, nubby cotton couches and chairs. The ceiling in the old house was high, and as the five of them warmed up, Anna noted that the acoustics were crisp and pleasing.

From the beginning things were different. Garrett looked to Anna to take the lead. Everyone sensed the shift in the order of things, but no one said a word. At one point, however, Anna caught Tom smiling privately to himself.

They rolled through the Schumann, movement by movement, without stopping. The balance sounded just right to Anna. Everything seemed to be working. In the silence that followed, Anna braced for the blast. Nothing came. She looked at Garrett who was looking directly at her. She shrugged and smiled. "I didn't know we could do that," she said.

Tom threw his head back and announced, "Wow!"

Clark said in his deliberate way, "That—was—fun."

Charlotte declared, "Better than yesterday, that's for sure."

"Well, it was certainly music," Garrett concluded. "Let's see what happens with the Brahms."

They stopped the Brahms halfway through for an exhaustive discussion of tempos and dynamics. Garrett didn't dictate, but he argued his points well. Tom, it turned out, had several good ideas. And Anna had a few other ideas from experiences with the piece in Boston. A consensus reached, they played the movement in question until they'd worked it out. Then finished off the work with gusto.

At five Garrett called a halt, pleading exhausted fingers. But then he asked them to stay on for tea or a drink. However, the Phillipses were eager to leave, saying they had to relieve their baby-sitter, and Tom confessed that he had a date. Which left Anna feeling rather awkward.

"I can stay for a little while, I guess. But my aunt's expecting me for dinner," she improvised brilliantly.

She stood by the window while Garrett saw the others out. She didn't turn around when he came back in. "Well, tea or sherry or what?"

"Tea's fine."

"Hot or iced?"

She turned and folded her arms across her chest. "I don't care. Whatever you're having."

"I'm having a small Scotch, neat."

"Oh. Well. I'll just go on then."

"Would you stay if I had tea?"

"Garrett, this is silly."

"For you to leave or for me to have tea?"

"This conversation is silly."

"I won't argue with that."

She stared at the small Navajo rug at her feet: beige with brown and one orange figure. "I should leave," she said.

"I'd like you to stay."

She looked up at him and nodded.

"I'll just go heat the water." He was moving toward the kitchen.

"Do you have any white wine?" she asked his back.

There was a pause, then his voice was muffled by the refrigerator. "Just happen to have about half a bottle of Chardonnay left from last night. Is that all right?"

"Fine."

He poked his head around the door. "Is it all right if I have Scotch?"

"Of course."

"Good. Then that's settled."

He brought the wine to her where she stood by the window, and sat down with a sigh on one edge of the large couch. "Cheers," he said. She echoed him. They each took a sip. A silence stretched out as Anna sat in a chair across from him.

"Well, how do you think it went?" he asked.

"Okay."

"Just okay?"

"I don't know. I figure my standards are weird or something. If I'd played that back in Boston I would have felt fantastic. As if we'd really done something wonderful. As it is, I just don't know what to think."

"It was fine."

"Do you really think so?"

"Hmm." He nodded, sipping his drink. "Oh, there're a few rough spots, but we've got the time we need, and it's going to be good. You were right. I needed to let go a bit."

She looked into her wineglass and couldn't think of a suitable reply. On the one hand, she would have liked to sit there forever, listening to his voice, his praise of their playing. On the other, she'd never been so acutely uncomfortable in her entire life.

"Tell me how it's going for you. I already know about your trouble with the conductor. But how's the rest of it? How're you getting on?"

She looked up into his smile. "Okay," she said.

"Just okay?"

"This sounds familiar. Let's see. Actually, everything is going pretty well. The house is great. The only thorn in my side, expect for said conductor, is Hal Corbett. I was warned. It's a lucky thing for him he's a good musician. Otherwise he'd be dead meat."

Garrett was laughing aloud. "That bad?"

"He's awful. He sways and leans and tries to poke me, I swear, with his bow. He even hums. Can't you hear him?"

"Sometimes," Garrett admitted through a grin. "I thought it was you."

"Thanks loads. But the rest of them are great. Charlotte is very nice to me. And Tom has turned out to be a good friend."

"Friends are important," he said thoughtfully. There was a pause. "But isn't he going out with the second oboist, Jan Darby? Last I heard, they were engaged."

"Oh. I don't know about that. I didn't mean that..."

"I know what you meant. But what about you?"

"What about me?"

"Are you involved with anyone these days?"

She couldn't read his expression. It seemed to convey nothing more than polite interest.

"I haven't been here very long," she reminded him, looking in confusion back into her wineglass, wondering how the conversation had taken this turn. "I'm just getting so I remember the names."

"What about back in Boston? Did you have any painful goodbyes?"

"If you mean what I think you mean, no. Not really."

"No room in your busy life for romance, eh?"

She lifted her chin. "Not even a second."

"You really ought to give it a chance. It's not so bad."

"You're hardly one to talk."

It had just come out. His eyes widened and her hand flew to her mouth. "I'm sorry. I didn't mean that."

"Oh? What exactly did you mean then?" He was pale beneath his tan and the polite smile had faded completely.

"Nothing. It just came out. I knew that . . . well, Simon told me about the divorce. But that was awful of me. Could we forget it?"

"I've been trying to for about a year now." He stood up and carried his drink to the piano. He sat down on the bench.

"I'm sorry," she repeated.

"Don't worry about it. Besides, you're quite right. I'm hardly one to give advice." He fingered a few notes, and then a chord. "I guess I was just saying that while getting involved with another person carries a risk, it has its rewards. Just because I made the wrong choice doesn't mean I won't try again. I'll just choose more carefully next time." He played with the chord, breaking it up into arpeggios.

She listened to the music with half an ear and heard herself say, "But sometimes it's not a question of choice. I mean, sometimes you just fall in love and there it is and it's the wrong person, but what can you do about it?"

He took his hands from the keyboard and looked over at her. "You can keep away from the person, I guess. Walk away from the situation before anything happens, before anyone gets hurt."

"What if you can't walk away? I mean, what if you work with the person or something, and have to see him all the time?"

"Sounds as if you're speaking from experience."

"Oh, no," she replied hastily, "not really. A friend's experience."

"Oh," he said, and gave her a steady look that brought her to her feet.

"I really ought to get going. Thanks for the wine."

She was already in the kitchen, putting her wineglass next to the shiny sink. All cream and oak with deep blue accents, the kitchen made her pause.

"Like it?" She turned to find him leaning against the doorjamb, his gray eyes light and warm.

She had to smile at him. "It's wonderful."

"I had it redone two years ago. We, that is, my ex-wife and I, both liked to cook." One side of his mouth lifted in a wry grin. "I think Sara regretted leaving the kitchen more than she regretted leaving me."

Before she thought, she put her hand on his brown arm. It was strong and warm, alive beneath her fingers. "I'm sorry," she whispered.

Those pale gray eyes. She felt as if she could disappear in them. They were so deep, so full of feeling, banked and smoldering.

"I promised myself," he answered evenly, "that if it ever happened again, I'd only get involved with a woman who'd never heard of melodic lines, who didn't have a clue what words like *vivace* or *andante* meant and couldn't tell a bassoon from a train."

"It sounds as if you should meet my Aunt Claire," Anna said carefully. "She'd be perfect for you."

Amusement flickered over his features. "I'll look forward to it."

The weekend passed in a blur of hard work. Thursday the orchestra was opening the Summer Festival by playing the first three of Bach's *Brandenburg* Concertos. Friday, they were playing the rest.

Anna was opening both concerts, as the violin soloist in the First and Fourth Concertos. The final rehearsals were intense, but Anna noticed that Garrett had shifted gears slightly. It was hard to put a finger on, but his attitude had changed. He was calling on his orchestra to work, not daring them to. He was suggesting, not demanding. He was substituting humor for sarcasm. Occasionally, he even smiled. By midweek Anna thought the music was going to ooze out of her pores.

It was after eleven on Wednesday night when Anna emerged from the hall, tired, preoccupied, annoyed to find it raining. She half ran to the bus shelter and huddled there, cursing her luck. She should have begged a ride home from someone. But everyone had been so tired and eager to leave. She'd stayed behind to work on a passage and now she was alone.

Footsteps sounded on the sidewalk. She felt a quaver of fear lurch through her stomach, then told herself to calm down. It was a public street. The footsteps stopped and she turned. About ten yards away she could see two rangy sets of blue-jeaned legs in two pairs of leather boots. The men both wore jean jackets, and one had a shaven head that glistened in the rain. She classified them as young toughs and turned to see if her bus was in sight. It wasn't.

"Hey!" one of them addressed her. She decided to ignore them. "Hey, I'm talkin' to you," he yelled, adding an unseemly epithet. It still seemed best to appear to ignore them.

She could hear the boots again, coming closer. They were talking loudly, between them, about her. She gripped her violin case firmly and turned to confront them.

"Leave me alone," she said in a loud voice.

"Whatcha gonna do, call the cops on your two-way wrist radio? Or izzat a machine gun you got there?"

The other said, "Hell, we just want some—ya know? But we're easy, we'll take anything ya got." They laughed heartily, and one of them hit the other loudly on the back. All the time they were closing in. The bald one wore a cascade of silver safety pins in his left earlobe. Anna doubted if either were over sixteen.

She realized too late her best defense would have been to run back into the Center where there were guards, people, help. She was trapped in the bus shelter now, cornered against the plastic walls. In an instant, life had changed into sheer terror. She saw a narrow space and bolted. She nearly made it around the barrier when she felt a strong grip on her shoulder throwing her back. It was the bald one who pinned her against the wall. His free hand went down to wrest the violin case from her hand.

Anna went wild. She twisted down to try to bite the wrist of the brutal hand and brought her knee up sharply. She missed with her teeth but she heard the man grunt as he released her to fall back, holding himself. His face was ugly as he glared and swore at her.

"Shut her up," he gasped as the hairy one lurched at her. She swung the violin case at him, but he grabbed and pulled at it. Anna was aware that the first one had recovered and was moving in again.

"That's enough. Back off. Let her go." Garrett's voice was loud and menacing and nearby. As the sound of it penetrated her consciousness, she realized she'd been screaming.

"Hey, man," said the hairy one, "we don't need this. Come on, man, let's split."

"Hey, man, we're just having a little fun," said the bald one, pushing the air with his hands as he backed away. "Keep your shirt on. You want her? She's yours." And then they both ran off up the street, laughing and pushing each other.

She stood there swaying, looking after them, breathing rapidly, her hand against her mouth, beyond anger or fear or any recognizable emotion. Garrett gently touched her shoulder and she turned, swinging out blindly before fully realizing who he was and sagging back against the plastic wall of the shelter.

"Anna," he murmured as he held her by the shoulders, "are you all right?"

She nodded and sagged against him. He held her there and gently took the heavy violin case from her hands.

"Was I screaming?"

"Loud enough to raise the dead. And fighting like a tiger. But, Anna, there were two of them. And they might have been armed."

At that moment a city bus wheezed to a stop next to them. The door popped and whistled open. The young Vietnamese driver leaned toward them, "Okay here? Wanna ride?"

Garrett shook his head and motioned him on and then began to guide Anna toward his car where he'd left it at the corner. They were nearly there when she said, "That was my bus."

"Right," he acknowledged. "But I'm giving you a ride."

He hadn't yet turned on the ignition when she yelled, "Dammit!"

"Are you all right?"

"I'm angry."

"But are you hurt?"

"No. Thanks to you. Oh, God. Thanks for being there." She looked out her side window, her lower lip caught in her teeth to stop it trembling.

"I'm glad I was. Though Lord knows I'm not much at playing Clint Eastwood. My hands aren't exactly registered as lethal weapons."

"You sounded pretty tough to me."

"I was trying to sound tough. And trying to figure out what I'd do if they called my bluff."

"They were kids."

"Punks. Probably on something. Looking for more. If they'd snagged your violin they would have been set for weeks."

She sank into the seat and moaned. "Don't."

"And if they'd had guns or . . ."

"Don't, Garrett, please. I'm already shaking all over. If I start in on the what ifs, I'll never sleep again."

He fell silent and pulled out into the street. Anna concentrated on her breathing and told herself it was over, she was all right. Nothing had happened. Garrett remained silent, and she felt she had to justify herself.

"I don't usually take a bus this late."

"I'm glad to hear it."

"I've never had any trouble before."

"Maybe you've been lucky."

"Oh, stop, Garrett."

"No, you listen. I didn't just happen by. I knew you'd stayed late and I came back to offer you a ride. A safe ride home. And you weren't there. So I figured you'd already gotten a ride. But the more I thought about it, the more uneasy I got. So when I left the lot I decided to cruise by the stop. And there you were." His voice was low and laden with repressed feeling.

"Then all I can do is thank you."

He went on. "I can't tell you how many times I've thought of you traipsing about the city at all hours with that lovely instrument dangling from your arm. I know you've been surviving on your own for a long time and are quite capable of taking care of yourself, but I couldn't keep myself from worrying."

She wasn't sure how to reply. She'd never given her own safety much thought. She was touched by his concern, but also miffed by his tone. He sounded like a father or a big brother admonishing her for foolish behavior. It was hard to admit he was right.

"I don't want you sleeping alone tonight."

She turned to his profile. "What?"

"Either I sleep at your house or you come to my house. And before you sputter indignities at me, I mean *sleep* in the very literal sense. I have no designs on your virtue. And I have two extra bedrooms. You're welcome to either. We're both exhausted. And I have a feeling you don't need to be alone tonight."

"You don't have to worry about me," she replied doggedly.

"You don't seem to understand, Anna. I *do* worry about you. That's what all this is about."

"But it's over. They're gone. Far away."

"That's true." He sighed as he took a sharp corner. "But, Anna, you'll be reliving the whole thing over and over, hearing noises, waiting. Whereas, perhaps if you're not alone, you'll feel a little more secure. Anyway, I'm in a mood to be humored."

"I think I'm too tired to argue."

"Thank goodness for that."

"I know I'd be perfectly all right by my..."

"I do, too. But let's just pretend this once you need somebody to take care of you."

Chapter Six

The light awoke her the next morning. The room was small, its walls off-white, its tall rectangular windows uncovered, its bed a single width pushed into a corner. There was a bookcase, a small teak dresser, a square bedside table that held a cobalt-blue gingerpot lamp and a tiny digital clock that read 7:03. Anna sat up.

The house was quiet. Unlike the raucous birds partying madly among the dogwood branches outside the open window. She'd slept through the night, a heavy, dreamless sleep for which she was grateful. Garrett had been right. She'd felt secure in his house. The menacing, monstrous boy-men only took shape in her mind's eye now, in the familiar light of day when they couldn't harm her.

Garrett had been so kind. He'd led her to his kitchen, sat her down at the table in the bay window and, though it was after midnight, fixed them both fluffy cheese omelets, buttery pieces of wheat toast, large cantaloupe wedges and tall glasses of grapefruit juice. As they ate he talked and kept her talking about the music, the concert, as if the other hadn't happened. When she'd finished eating, he handed her a stubby glass that held a fraction of an inch of brandy and she tipped it back at his order, warming her body from throat to toes, fuzzing the margins of her brain.

As she handed him back the glass, their fingers brushed lightly against each other. Anna closed her eyes now against the brilliant morning light and recalled the feeling of that brief, warm touch. And how she responded by stretching up on her tiptoes and kissing his cheek quickly on the soft warm skin at the side of his cheek just above the line of his beard. His hands went to her shoulders and he held her there, his gray eyes solemnly on her. "Thank you," she whispered.

That made him smile. "Come on. I'll show you your room." He found an unused toothbrush and gave her an oversize T-shirt to use as a nightgown. As she crawled between the heavy white sheets she could hear his quiet movements downstairs, water running in the kitchen, the hum of the refrigerator. Then she heard the bolting of a door. And that was all she remembered.

She threw back the covers and walked across the satiny wood floor to the window. It faced south and looked over the garden and the front walk. She opened the door quietly and tried to remember the way to the bathroom. There was a closed door to the left and one directly across the hallway that was slightly ajar. She stepped through it and found herself in Garrett's empty room. She almost ducked out again but then decided one look wouldn't hurt.

The room was large, with windows on two walls. Set on the diagonal in the corner opposite Anna was a large brass bed neatly covered with a navy down coverlet. The pale blue-gray walls were full of watercolors of sailboats resplendent with bright spinnakers. In the corner to the left of the doorway was a large navy leather chair with a full bookcase on one side and a table and brass reading lamp on the other.

She breathed him in deeply. Feeling emboldened, Anna crossed to the window between the chair and the bed. Beyond the veil of Japanese maple leaves lay Queen Anne Hill and Lake Union. As she watched, a seaplane, glinting in the sunlight, spiraled up out of the lake and headed north over the flat University District.

She heard a creaking sound and turned to see Garrett striding into the room, stripping a sweat-stained T-shirt from his back. It was hanging from his elbows before he looked up and saw her. He made an obvious effort not to laugh outright at her discomfort as he nonchalantly tossed the shirt onto the floor and said, "Hullo? Awake, then?"

She looked at him standing there: his grinning face, flushed from exercise; his bare chest tan and gleaming, lean and powerful, the light brown hairs dense at his heart, then disappearing until they regrouped at his belly and descended into the waistband of his brief red shorts; the long, strongly corded legs. There was not an inch of fat on him. Nothing but muscle and power. The hard knot of desire that had lain hidden deep in Anna, semidormant, almost forgotten, surged and struggled against her reason. She swallowed hard and addressed a point past his left ear. "You caught me snooping."

"Find anything interesting?"

"I was looking for the bathroom."

"There's one right there through that door, but it's mine and I'm about to use the shower. Yours is the next door down, on this side of the hall. I put towels out for you."

She tried to move and failed. She could smell him. A smell like the room's, only alive, vibrantly alive and oddly intoxicating, and Anna felt something move and give at the center of her soul. Somewhere, some part of her wanted to leave the room quickly, get away, get to someplace else, far away from what she was feeling. But she couldn't. After a long pause, her brain kicked feebly into gear. "Did you have a good run?" she asked, and congratulated herself on her casual tone.

He pulled his fingers through his damp hair. "Actually, I didn't leave the house. I was in the cellar. I've got a kind of gym rigged up down there. For when it rains, you know."

"It's not raining."

"No. I guess I didn't want to leave you alone here. In a strange place."

"Oh."

"Did you sleep well?"

"Yes. Thanks."

"Good." He was standing there, shiny with sweat, legs slightly apart, his hands resting lightly at his hips, flaunting himself. She wished she could stop trembling, stop the sensations that flowed and flamed over and through her, that threatened to buckle her knees.

"Nice nightgown you're wearing. Very becoming."

"Garrett..."

"Yes, ma'am."

Her voice could barely leave her throat. She swallowed. "I feel kind of foolish."

"Why?"

"Why do you think?"

"Tell me."

"You're half naked and I'm standing here in your T-shirt."

"So?"

She shivered. "Don't make fun of me."

"I'm not." There was a silence. She could hear him breathing. She could almost feel his pulse. She could not look at him. His voice when he spoke was so low it seemed to come from far away. "You're trembling." She looked at him then and found that his brows were furrowed and his eyes dark and serious. "You're afraid of me, aren't you?"

"I don't trust you," she whispered. She couldn't tell him she didn't trust herself.

His eyes flashed. "Now that's not fair. Anna. All previous promises aside, do you honestly think I would...oh, God, do anything after what happened to you last night? Do you think I don't know how awful and disgusting that whole business was for you?"

"You've been very kind and I'm grateful..."

"Oh, damn grateful!" he exploded, then added more softly, "I don't want your gratitude."

"I can't give you what you want."

"You don't know what I want, Anna."

"I'd better go now."

He drew a great breath and let it out in a rush. "Sure. Yes. Go." And he turned away from her.

Twenty minutes later Anna carefully descended the bare wooden steps into the kitchen. The coffee smelled deliciously strong. Garrett was seated at the round white table by the window where they'd eaten their omelets.

He looked up as she came into the room. His eyes were grave.

"May I start over again?" she asked, consciously smiling.

He stood up and his eyes lightened. "No need. I'm to blame. I never can say the right things to you, somehow." She turned away to pour herself a mug of coffee and splashed milk into it as he sat back down and went on, "I'm always keyed up the day of a concert. It gets worse as the day goes on, I'm afraid."

"This looks good," she said as she sat down to a wedge of honeydew on a white plate. She looked up at him. "You do take very good care of me."

"Anna."

"Yes?"

"Can you tell me something?"

"I can try."

"Why don't you have a car?"

It was such a different question from the one she expected, that for the second time that morning she was caught off guard. "It's never been necessary. In Boston, a car was a nuisance."

"In Seattle, I'm afraid, it's a necessity."

"I really don't want one. I don't like to drive. I can manage," she added defensively.

He was silent for a moment. "Could you have managed last night?"

"That's never happened before," she said quickly.

"Do you think it might never happen again?"

"Cars aren't safe, either."

"Hold it. That's another argument."

"Why do we have to argue?"

"We don't. You seem to want to," he pointed out.

"Honestly, you don't have to worry about me. I got careless last night. I'm not usually careless. And I'll certainly be more careful after this. I was very lucky you were there...."

"Forget all that. I'm thinking about that morning you were late. What are you planning to tell me when you're late for a performance?"

"That won't happen."

"Not if I can help it. I've been thinking. Until you get yourself a car, I'll do what I can to get you around."

"What?"

"Think of me as a taxi. At least as far as music is concerned. I draw the line at delivering you for a clandestine rendezvous, et cetera, but..."

"Garrett..."

"I'm perfectly serious. I have a hell of a lot on my mind, and I don't want to add the extra burden of wondering where on earth my concertmaster is and whether or not she's going to make it to the concert. So I'll drive you. End of discussion."

"I'll move closer to the Center."

"Fine. Until then, I drive you."

She could feel the heat rise in her neck. "I don't want to depend on you."

"You don't seem to understand. *I* depend on *you*. To be where you're supposed to be, when you're supposed to be."

She bit down on her lip and sat very still with her hands in her lap, her melon untasted. He reached a hand over the table toward her. "Please don't fight me on this."

Anna took refuge in silence. She found that Garrett would fill in the blanks if she said nothing. He changed the subject and talked about the evening's concert as her brain and emotions churned. Twenty minutes after breakfast he was driving her home. He wasn't taking the direct route. As they climbed off the main arterial she realized he was taking Interlaken Road, which would deposit them after many twists and turns into the Arboretum. She watched the houses and trees go by in silence and was not surprised when he turned onto the inner road of the Arboretum to park. He turned off the ignition and looked at her.

"It's a beautiful morning for a walk. Do you mind?" Without waiting for her answer he was out and opened her door. Silently she walked away from him down the path toward the hill. The trees were huge Douglas firs, the rhododendron densely green. She heard him say her name but didn't turn. He touched her arm and she flinched away.

"Anna, what is it?"

Now she turned. "It's you."

"Now what have I done?"

She looked at him steadily and told him. "You've taken over my professional life. And now you're trying to take over the rest. First you tell me how to play music. Fine, that's okay. But now you tell me how to live my life. I need space between us and you close it up. I don't mean to sound ungrateful, Garrett. I appreciate what you did for me last night. And maybe you don't mean to be so overbearing... I don't know. I'm confused. But I need my independence. My self-respect. I'll manage my own transportation."

He stood with his hands at his sides. "Overbearing, eh?" he said, his mouth tilted.

"Yup," she affirmed with her chin high, her eyes flashing.

He shoved his hands in his pockets and strolled thoughtfully past her before he turned back. "You're absolutely right, of course. You seem to bring out my not-so-latent protective tendencies."

She folded her arms. "Perhaps you should adopt a puppy."

"Ouch."

"Just a suggestion."

He sighed. "Listen, what if I just request that you take a few reasonable precautions, at least think about buying your own car and please not hesitate to ask me if you need a ride. Is that still overbearing?"

"It's better."

He nodded, apparently satisfied. "Good. That's a relief. Will you walk with me then? There's this duck family I'd like to visit at the pond. The babies are probably teenagers now, and I've been wondering how they're getting on."

He wore a white formal jacket for the concert. He looked devastating, but rigid with tension, remote, impenetrable. Their leisurely walk in the Arboretum might never have happened. He acknowledged her existence with a nod and a "you didn't call me."

"The Phillipses drove me," she admitted.

"As long as you're here." And then he was gone, making his rounds of the sections, speaking briefly to each principal, and probably not hearing their responses. She knew he was listening to the music inside himself, that he wouldn't emerge from his mood until the concert was over.

Minutes later Anna was waiting backstage to make her first entrance as concertmaster of the Northwest Symphony. The orchestra quit its doodling and went quiet in anticipation. She nodded to the manager to open the door and she strode out, her black skirt swishing gracefully at her ankles, her violin held firmly by the neck. The applause came as a pleasant surprise. It seemed warm and welcoming, and she smiled at it as she'd seen Simon do so many times before. In another few moments she'd seen to the tuning of the orchestra. Then Garrett arrived, the soloists took their places and they were launched on Bach's First *Brandenburg* Concerto.

All the ugly and tumultuous events of the past twenty-four hours fell away from Anna as she played. She linked up with a civilized past as she fingered Bach's perfect notes with skill and finesse. She transmitted through the music all that was fine and good about human beings and left behind all that was evil and devious.

Garrett, as he conducted her, was no longer an adversary, a complicated, passionate, domineering man who confused and dismayed and attracted her all at the same time; he was simply the conductor, the person who led them through the intricate, wonderful music of the master.

Backstage when it was over, she emerged from a bear hug bestowed by an elated Tom MacMahon to find herself eye to eye with Garrett. He was nodding at her slowly, his mouth in a funny line. "Not too bad for a beginner," he said very seriously.

"Don't overdo it, Garrett," Tom counseled. "She may faint from the shock."

He looked at him. "That was nice work on the cello, Tom."

Tom placed a fluttering hand to his chest and murmured, "Be still, my heart. Can it be true?"

"Don't let it go to your head," Garrett added. "There's still tomorrow night."

"Tote that barge, lift that bale," Tom intoned as he saluted and turned on his heel to leave.

Garrett's gaze followed the young man as he marched away. "Something tells me," he said after a moment, "that I forget to dwell on the positive." He looked at Anna for confirmation.

"Perhaps. But you get good results from your criticism."

He began to turn away then stopped. "May I give you a ride home?"

"You don't have to."

"I know. But I'd like to. I have a few things I'd like to discuss with you."

In another fifteen minutes they were installed in Garrett's Jaguar, and it was dawning on Anna that he was again taking a very long and circuitous route to her house in Madrona. He drove at a stately pace through the Arboretum and then turned left toward Madison Park and Lake Washington. If she had expected him to take up the difficult themes of earlier in the day, she was mistaken. For he was intent on dissecting the concert piece by piece. She became so involved in listening and adding her own thoughts to his, that she didn't even notice when he pulled into a parking place down by the lake and switched off the engine.

He stretched his arm across the back of her seat and turned to her. "Now, tell me how you think you did," he said.

She immediately tensed. "Is this a test?"

"Perhaps."

"I think . . . well, it could have been better in spots. But I thought the section worked well. I felt confident, sure of the notes. And I think the solo went...pretty well." He was grinning. "Did I give the right answer?"

"Anna, Anna. Sometimes I think we're maybe too much alike. Too self-critical by half. Of course, it can always be better, since perfection is impossible on this earth. But you gave me what I'd hoped to hear and more." The only possible reply to this was silence. She became aware that one finger was insinuating itself among the curls at her neck. "Yes. Very pleased." She stopped breathing for a moment, conscious of their proximity in the small car, of the suddenly charged atmosphere. Then abruptly he removed his arm and placed his hands on the wheel. "Now tell me how I did."

Her wits scrambled. "You mean as a conductor?"

"Yes. As a conductor. What else? I seem to remember that quite recently you had a lot to say about my conducting. Among other things. I just wondered how I measured up."

She felt embarrassed. "Garrett."

"Go ahead. I can take it."

"You were terrific."

"I won't settle for that."

Of course he wouldn't. "I think, in spite of what I said before, you communicate with an orchestra better than any conductor I've ever worked with. Especially in performance. Some are fine in rehearsal but can't seem to pull it off under pressure. You are inclined to be awfully wordy and rather negative in rehearsal, but in performance, you're...well, very clear, very precise, very consistent. As if it's right there in your head."

"It is," he said simply. "I put it there." He thought for a moment. "I take it, then, that I really need to load on the praise."

"No. I was wrong about that. Maybe you just need to remember that we're all there for the same reason."

He was silent for a time. "I never asked you. Did San Francisco offer you a job?"

She blinked in surprise. "Yes, in fact. The day after you did."

"Do you regret not taking it?"

She swallowed but didn't drop her gaze from his in the dim light. "There have been times. But right now, I'm glad I'm here."

"So am I," she heard him say just before he started the engine.

They drove in silence the rest of the way to her house, following the weaving road that led past large houses and along the black lake where no moon reflected in the waves. The car climbed smoothly up the hill and nudged in at the curb by Anna's house.

"Thanks for letting me bring you home."

"Thanks for understanding what I was trying to say this afternoon."

"May I have the honor of escorting you tomorrow evening?"

She sighed in exasperation. "I don't think it's good for the entire orchestra to see us coming and going together."

"Oh, so that's it."

"Partly."

"Some people might say we spent the night together last night. They wouldn't be lying exactly. But on the other hand, it wasn't my idea of a . . ."

"Don't."

"All I'm saying is that people are going to talk, no matter what the truth is. You're not going to be able to prevent it."

"So why make it worse?"

"How do you define worse? You've made it quite clear to me that you don't want to get involved. That you want 'space,' as you put it, between us. I respect your wishes. I don't think I actually agree with them," he added with a little tug to his earlobe, "but I respect them. But if the rest of the world wants to..."

She glared at him. "You are the most maddening man I've ever met."

He smiled maddeningly. "Thank you." And he walked her to her door.

Once inside she tried to gather her scattered wits about her. Being with Garrett Downing was like reeling from one extreme emotion to another: from rage to laughter, from frustration to gratitude, from something very close to love to something frighteningly near hate.

She ran a hot bath in the old porcelain tub and wished as always that it were a little longer and deeper. She settled herself as comfortably as possible into the steaming water laced liberally with fragrant oil and closed her eyes. Love and hate. How could she even think in those terms? She'd laid the ground rules herself: no involvement with the management. But everything was shifting around so quickly now. That morning. He'd stood there and simply showed her his body while she'd quivered in anticipation of something she told herself she didn't want and could never understand, all the while knowing—sensing, rather—that if he moved toward her, that if he took one step and asked, she wouldn't be able to resist.

Her eyes clicked open. Consequences. She had to think about the consequences of that sort of thing. She'd known a lot of women who'd thrown away so much in the name of just what she was feeling now. It didn't matter whether you called it lust or love. What mattered was what happened when it had burned itself out.

All these years Anna had been intelligent enough to fend off the sort of ardor that would play havoc with her well-ordered life. When casual friendships threatened to heat up, she'd backed away from them and won for her wisdom a reputation as standoffish and stuck-up. But what had resulted in loneliness had also paid off in excellence in her work. She'd graduated with honors. And look at her now, a concertmaster and not yet twenty-six. And she didn't get there by sleeping with her professors or her conductors.

Or with anyone else.

She drew up her knees, thinking the old familiar thoughts. It was embarrassing, in this day and age, to be as old as she was and still a virgin. She tried to picture herself telling the truth to Garrett and winced at the image of his amazed amusement.

Of course, she had never felt for any man what she had experienced with Garrett. She'd never felt anything in her life like what she'd experienced with Garrett. Desire so potent that it numbed the brain and reduced her to a single sensation: want.

And yet, and yet. She had put it aside effectively, had forgotten all about it, had played the music, had survived the day and the long ride home with him next to her, hadn't embarrassed herself, hadn't compromised herself. She'd been able to talk to him rationally, reasonably. What was more, she'd been listened to. And wasn't that far more important than a mere love affair?

One day at a time, she counseled herself as she slipped into her nightgown and robe. She knew the warning signs now. She could stay in control. She could be friends. She could even like him.

And that realization made her smile. For she did like him. His off-center sense of humor, the lopsided grin that warmed his cool eyes, his ability to see through to the center of an idea, his intelligence, his mastery of his art, his covert bursts of generosity, his deep core of vulnerability. His loneliness. She could forgive him his moods, his remoteness; she understood them. He was a perfectionist, like her. When he made music, he was totally absorbed by it and nothing was allowed to intrude.

The telephone woke her up early the next morning. "Anna, it's Charlotte. Did I wake you?"

"What is it?"

"I'm sorry. The baby got me up early. I forget other people can sleep. Have you seen the paper?"

"No. I don't even take it."

"Well, listen up. Front page. 'Who is she?' "

"What . . . ?"

"Shhhhh. Listen. First page of the Arts section. 'Young Woman Makes Debut in NWSO. Concertmistress Anna Terhune claimed the Seattle Center Concert Hall stage for her own last night from the very first note. A Seattle native, Terhune returned to take over the first chair this month and made a ravishing debut as the violin soloist in Bach's First *Brandenburg*. She returns tonight to solo in the first work of the evening, the Fourth *Brandenburg* Concerto. She is not to be missed.' "

"Charlotte, you're making this up."

"No, darling. I'd say this reporter is seriously in love. He went on for another three paragraphs before some editor cut him off. Can't wait to see what he makes of tonight."

The house was full, and backstage the word was there were people demanding standing-room tickets. Anna was warming up in a corner when she looked up to see Garrett watching her.

"Don't let it go to your head," he said.

"Never," she replied. "The guy is loony."

He raised an eyebrow. "The 'guy' is sixty-five and knows his music, Anna."

"I won't let it go to my head."

"Fine."

At the end of the Fourth, she felt wonderful. By the end of the Fifth, she was ready to take on the world. When the Sixth finally ended, she was exhausted. But people came backstage to shake her hand. She talked and smiled until she thought her face would break. The Phillipses offered her a drive home, so she turned Garrett down, then spent the final minutes before sleep regretting it. She wanted to know what he thought. She'd seen his quiet smile, but she wanted to hear his words.

Meanwhile there was work to do, music to play and lots of it. The reviewer was ecstatic over Anna's performances in the Bach in his second review, and she began to discover the taste of fame. Three fan letters found their way into her mail slot. And one proposal. From a nine-year-old violin student. She answered them all carefully.

Garrett said nothing about the review. In fact, Garrett had intruded very little on her life since that long night and day they'd spent together. He'd popped into quartet rehearsals, continued working rigorously on the quintets, to be performed that weekend, and had honed the piano/violin sonatas to something approaching perfection. Even when they'd been alone, rehearsing the sonatas, he'd been distant—pleasant, but distant. He seemed guarded, almost cautious. Several times she looked at him to find him looking away.

And several times Anna caught herself simply wanting nothing so much as to touch him. Staring at the fine laugh wrinkles at the corner of his eye or at the hollow of his neck or at the eloquent curve of his wrist, she would be so overwhelmed by her physical need for him that she nearly reached out her hand. She never did, and after a while, her heartbeat would subside and reason would regain its hold on her. Every time it happened she felt humiliated and confused. She told herself that time would cure her obsession.

They performed the piano quintets to an enthusiastic crowd who applauded until the five musicians granted an encore by repeating a movement from the Brahms. As Anna shared the applause with Tom and the Phillipses and Garrett, as the five of them grinned at one another with their color high and their eyes dancing, she felt an intoxicating surge of well-being. They really were all equals in each other's eyes at that moment. They'd shared in the recreation of two magnificent musical works. They'd shaped them and translated them and performed them well. And Anna felt a part of it.

Later when the rest of them wanted to go celebrate with a drink, she let herself go along. Tom's friend Jan joined them, as well, which paired Anna with Garrett. The conversation was buoyant and full of self-congratulation that even Garrett didn't try to dissipate. But he did notice Anna's silence beside him.

"How did we do, professor?" he asked her with a grin.

"We did good," she answered with a forced heartiness. Just sitting next to him in the crowded booth had sapped her energy.

"Can I give you a lift home?"

"The Phillipses are driving me, thanks."

"I could talk them out of it."

"Please don't," she pleaded in a low voice. "Don't spoil this."

He had to respond to something Tom was saying before he turned back to her. "Who's driving you to Port Gamble tomorrow for our little three o'clock matinee at the community church, hmm?"

"I checked the bus schedule and..."

He laughed at her before saying pointedly, "I'm picking you up at eleven, and that is all there is to that."

She said the only words she could. "Thanks."

"Even if you had a car, Anna, it would be silly for us both to drive."

His tone had changed and she looked at him. "I know. I'm sorry."

"Anna," Clark said as he leaned across the thickly varnished plank that served as a table, "why is it you don't have a car like the rest of us? You unAmerican or something?"

"No. I guess I'll have to give in and get one. It's silly not to, and a nuisance. I just...well—" And the words tumbled out. "My mother was killed in a wreck. I was in the car, too, and I wasn't hurt, but I'm not too wild about cars or driving."

A silence descended on the table. Anna felt acutely uncomfortable. Aware once more that she was different, that she was odd, that she always stood apart from everyone. She laughed a little hoarsely. "It's not very logical, but . . ."

"But very understandable," Garrett finished quietly.

Clark murmured an apology and the conversation jerked and spurted until it settled on the less emotional topic of future concerts.

Outside in the warm night, Garrett waited with Charlotte and Anna while Clark got the car. Tom and Janet had already left. "Clothes," Anna said suddenly, turning to Garrett. "You haven't mentioned clothes. Do you want me like this, in a long black skirt?"

It was a steady look, but his eyes danced with pent-up emotion. He finally had to look away before he answered. "Don't wear black. Bring something pretty and colorful. For a Sunday afternoon in a church sanctuary. But don't wear it in the car. You can change when we get there."

Chapter Seven

Anna woke up quickly Sunday morning, excited and apprehensive all at the same time. After a shower and cup of coffee she took a deep breath and plunged into her closet to find something suitable for the concert that afternoon. She and Garrett. All by themselves.

She finally settled on a simple dress, a paisley print of cool pastels, loosely waisted, that fell to below her knees in a fullish skirt. She pressed the lace collar and put the dress into a plastic garment bag, then packed her underthings, shoes and makeup in her duffel. She put on her jeans and a comfortable, overlarge cotton shirt, grabbed a light sweater and settled down to wait.

She'd never seen him in blue jeans before, but he was wearing them when he came to her door, jeans and a red polo shirt. He carried her things to his car as she bolted her front door. She saw her dress nestled next to his dark suit on the rack and took her place in the passenger seat. Garrett had said nothing. He had dark smudges beneath his eyes.

"How are your nerves?" she asked him quietly after they were underway.

"Ridiculously rotten," he answered. "How are you?"

"About the right amount of tense, I guess."

They were both silent, then he asked, "Does just riding in a car bother you?"

She realized abruptly why he'd understood so readily last night. He was something of an expert himself on irrational fears. "Sometimes," she replied. "I do a lot of gasping, especially on a freeway." She hesitated then asked, "Are you afraid performing the sonatas will be too much like performing alone?"

She looked at his profile and saw a slow smile lift his face. "When you put it like that, I realize how crazy it sounds."

"There's nothing crazy about nerves or fear, Garrett. They're a part of life."

"How did you know about my particular fear, though?"

"Something Simon told me. How you quit. And didn't ever go back to it. Until now. And even now, well, you're not scheduled to play any solo recitals."

He drove in silence for a time, but she knew he was mulling something over, deciding whether to speak. They were on the freeway cruising north before he began. "When I was sixteen I was performing a series of recitals in Paris. This particular day—I remember it was May 11—I was supposed to play an all Chopin program. I knew the stuff well and had played most of it a million times. But I got up there and my brain went blank. Nothing. As if it just shut off. I sat very still for what seemed like an eternity. I could hear the audience rustling and coughing. Then I just stood up and walked off again. And never went back."

"It must have been awful," Anna murmured.

"It was, I suppose. Of course it was. Like looking into a dark hole. But in a way, it was wonderful, too. It meant it was all over. No one could force me back into that life. It was hell, Anna," he finished bluntly.

"What about your parents?"

"What about them?"

"Where were they?"

"They lived in London. I hadn't lived with them in nearly ten years. I guess I was rather a surprise all around, and they really didn't know what to do about me from the moment I arrived. My mother was forty-five when I was born, my father sixty. I was their first and last. When it became obvious that I had this talent, they gave me over to the man who was to manage my career for the next ten years. I lived with him and his wife. They were decent to me, and I had the best teachers and tutors. But I only saw my parents on holidays. My father died when I was eight. My mother passed away last year. A stroke. The last time I saw her she didn't know me."

Anna was silent, saddened, and Garrett asked gently, "How old were you when your mother was killed?"

"Nine."

"That must have been difficult."

"It was so sudden. Everything just kind of turned upside down. We were very close, I think, for mother and daughter, though we were very different. We used to have long talks. She made me feel very loved, very secure. I hate it now that I can't remember her face or her voice. I can't remember the accident at all. I think I just blocked it." Garrett said nothing. "My father died my last year of high school. A heart attack, they said."

"I remember meeting him once or twice. You must have been very close to him, especially after..."

"No I wasn't. I know it seems as if I should have been. But it wasn't that way. I didn't really even see much of him. He was a surgeon, so he could keep busy. He was good about coming to my concerts and recitals, and I think he was proud of me. But my mother's death just wiped him out emotionally. It was like he didn't have anything left over. And I was just a reminder. Though he never really said he wished I'd been the one killed."

"Anna..." Garrett interjected, horrified.

"It's all right. I sorted it all out long ago." She'd had to, she thought to herself, or she wouldn't have made it this far. She knew she sounded cold, removed, dispassionate. But she couldn't help it.

Garrett spoke after a moment. "It seems that both of us are too familiar with loneliness. We've had to make our own lives, one way or the other. Perhaps we were fortunate, in a way, in having music to disappear into. Perhaps if your life had been different you might never have pursued a career in music. I nearly gave it up completely. But after a few years of wandering around the map, I realized I couldn't. It was too much a part of me. Conducting was a revelation, something completely mine, but something involving . . . I can't explain it. The feeling I get when I conduct. It's power, I suppose. I'm in control, but there's so much more involved. I suppose conducting gives me what I never had before. A feeling of communion, of community."

He was silent for a moment. "And I still have my damned nerves, as you well know. Even though nothing has ever happened, I've never blanked out, not even briefly. My nerves remind me to be careful, to stay in control, to trust myself."

"So you think I ought to go ahead and get a car?"

He glanced at her. "Yes, I do. Though I can't deny the danger. You see that idiot who just swerved in ahead of that car? Another fraction of an inch and we would all be piling into each other right now." He let out a breath then added, "If I did freeze up in a concert, I wouldn't die of it. Driving is different from playing a piano. Or conducting a symphony."

"But fear is fear."

In the silence that followed, Anna felt her body relax. She took several deep breaths, just enjoyed the feeling. This, perhaps, was happiness. "I like you, Garrett," she said softly.

He darted a sideways look of surprise at her.

"I just wanted you to know. When you're like this. Kind. Understanding. When you're not pushing me and hinting at things. When it's like this, it feels as if maybe we really could be friends."

He didn't answer her.

The ferry, wide-hulled, shiny white, was full of Sunday travelers: harried families keeping track of excited children, oblivious couples leaning on the rail with arms entwined, determined campers with heavy boots and many-tiered backpacks, lean-limbed bicyclists in slick shorts, foreign tourists armed with maps and cameras.

"Do you suppose we're the only ones working this afternoon?" came Garrett's voice by her ear.

Anna tilted her head toward him until it came to rest against the solid warmth of his upper arm. In the moment that followed he put his arm around her and pulled her in close to his side. Reflexively, she looped her arm around his waist and rubbed her cheek against the soft redness of his shirt, and felt the deep steady rhythm of his heart. It was like the dance they'd danced. It felt absolutely right. It was as if her body had been shaped to fit against his. But this time, the music didn't end.

Together, in silent contentedness, they leaned against the rail and watched the always greedy, ever watchful, raucous gulls swooping and crying overhead. The sun shone brightly through the brisk breeze. In the west the Olympic Mountains stood out in relief against a bank of glowering clouds.

Then the ferry docked and they were in the car again, talking over the music and the order of the concert. Too soon they arrived at the outskirts of tiny Port Gamble and pulled into the parking lot next to its delicately Victorian community church. Once the car was stopped, the ignition off, something of Garrett's previous tension returned. She gave him a brave smile he couldn't return.

The chairwoman of the Port Gamble Arts Committee welcomed them at the door in a flutter of lavender organdy, plump hands, powder and floral scent.

Anna and Garrett took turns changing into their concert clothes in a small room off the sanctuary. He smiled distractedly at her dress and murmured "nice," and she straightened his wine-red tie and smiled back. She knew she was as eager to play as he was to forget the whole thing.

Once they entered the sanctuary, the performer in Garrett took over. Anna listened in amazement as he charmingly addressed the ninety-eight souls who had turned out that afternoon. He told them about the Summer Festival and about that afternoon's recital, explaining briefly the sonata form, revealing telling bits about the composers. They were playing Brahms's First Sonata, then a short Schubert romance, and then, after a brief intermission, Franck's one and only sonata: all examples of romanticism—lushly melodic, richly lyrical, profoundly emotional. "And who better to perform these beautiful pieces with," he concluded, "than Anna Terhune, Northwest Symphony's beautiful new concertmaster." He kissed her hand, smiling at the color rising in her cheeks, and several matrons patted their hands together ecstatically.

The piano might have been in better tune, it was true. And the rain might have held off another hour instead of clattering down on the shake roof halfway through the Schubert. But Anna played as she never had before. And they played together as they never had in rehearsal. Their communication was absolute, and the result was electric.

The ninety-eight members of the audience listened attentively, and if they occasionally applauded between movements, the musicians forgave them and used the time to retune and exchange looks. When it was over Anna and Garrett stood with their hands locked together and smilingly bowed as one. The enthusiastic applause died abruptly as a thunder clap rattled the leaded windows and lightning dimmed the slightly swaying chandeliers. Then the chairwoman of the Entertainment Committee thanked the musicians and invited everyone to stay for punch and cookies.

Anna felt Garrett's involuntary, inaudible sigh of resignation and then heard him accept with pleasure. "Good P.R.," he whispered in her ear as he led her down the stairs. So for a half hour they drank fruit punch and ate homemade cookies, accepted compliments and smiled a lot. They heard how "lovely" the music sounded, "what an attractive couple" they made and "how nice" they were to come all that way to play such pretty songs.

By half past five they were back in their jeans and back in the car. Garrett was trying to navigate the road as the windshield wipers beat furiously and impotently against the torrential rain. He hadn't said much since they'd pulled out of the church lot, and Anna hesitated to break in on his concentration.

"Do you need to get back right away?" he asked abruptly, without preface.

"What do you mean?"

"To Seattle? Do you care if we go back right away?"

"I suppose not," she said warily. "Why?"

He cursed the car bearing down on them without headlights. "I thought, if you didn't mind, we could check on my little house on Bainbridge Island."

"What little house on Bainbridge Island?"

"Mine." He smiled at her. "It's just a cottage, really. Just a place I go when I've had it with the city. I've got a piano there, and a small sailboat. It's a bit of a drive yet, but not much farther than we'd have to drive anyway. And anything is better than a ferry crossing in this muck." She was still thinking it over when he went on. "I haven't been able to get there for two or three weeks. I guess I should have mentioned it before," he finished lamely.

"But you wanted to wait until it would be difficult for me to refuse."

He flashed a look at her, then turned his attention back to the road. "Actually, I was going to mention it before, but you seemed so at ease and I didn't want to ruin your mood." He waited. "Would you mind it so dreadfully? Spending a little more time with me?"

She sighed heavily. "Since you put it that way. If you have to check your house, we'll check your house."

"We could pick up some food on the way and cook dinner."

"I'm not sure about the 'we' part, since cooking is not exactly my forte. But I am hungry."

"Me, too," he agreed. "Can't eat much before a concert and I'm ravenous afterwards."

"How do you think it went?"

"I thought..." he began, and drew it out until it fell into a silence. He breathed, then his low voice picked up the thread. "I thought it was magical. Playing that music with you this afternoon was an extraordinary experience. I know you felt it, too. We were a totality. It so rarely happens like that. Even the best of our rehearsals hadn't prepared me for it."

She felt the words blaze a warm and lighted pathway through her brain. "Do you suppose anyone there felt it?"

"I know they were quiet and we had them with us all the way. That in itself on a rainy summer afternoon is an accomplishment. But what I felt inside, Anna..." He stopped. "Damn," he whispered, and paused again. "We were so close. Just you and me and that exquisite music. It was like nothing so much as making love to you."

Anna's sense of well-being, the extreme pleasure she'd felt as his words had drifted around her, vanished in a flash of something close to anger. "Just what am I supposed to say to that?" she asked him tightly.

"I was hoping you'd agree with me," he replied, tension edging his voice. "You can't tell me you felt nothing. That you feel nothing, Anna."

At that moment she couldn't tell him anything. Her hands twisted in her lap and she looked blindly into the darkness speeding by. There were too many wars going on in her mind and body. Her physical desire for him was so real that she ached. Her need for his friendship, for his approval, for his mere presence was a craving she'd been conscious of for days or weeks or maybe years. And the experience she'd just shared with him, the indescribable experience of playing beautiful music, of communicating flawlessly, of linking their musical instruments in a sort of rapturous bond—if, indeed, as he said, it was like making love, then perhaps there was no point in denying the situation any longer.

But. Always a voice in Anna's head cried out "But!" He was still who he was, Garrett Downing, her conductor, her boss, older, more experienced, off limits. She could like him, she could play music with him, but she couldn't have an affair with him. If she fell in love with him—and she knew she was more than half in love with him already—where would that leave her? In a complete and total mess. No self-respect, no peace, no..."

"Anna, say something at least."

"There's nothing to say."

"I think there's a great deal. I think it's time for us to talk about it. It's not just going to go away. God knows I've tried to make it go away. It just won't."

She nearly asked him what in the world he was talking about. It was tempting to fall back on that, play it innocent and naive. But she knew exactly what he was talking about and also knew that if she asked, he wouldn't hesitate to spell it out in so many words. She drew a deep breath and blew it out slowly. "I'm not ready to talk about it, Garrett. I don't plan on ever being ready. It's not something I want to discuss with you at any time. I thought I'd made that abundantly clear. Anything else, but not that. Please."

It was Garrett's turn to be silent. In silence he veered into the parking lot of a convenience store. He ran through the wet and disappeared for a few minutes as Anna sat in the car, listening to the steady fall of rain, to the occasional muted whoosh of cars passing on the road, to her confused thoughts. For a brief moment she entertained the possibility of simply running away. Getting out of the car and making her own way back.

She peered through the sheets of rain and realized she didn't even know where she was.

Without a word Garrett got back into the car and drove on through the wet, darkening evening. At last they entered the outskirts of the Bainbridge Island town of Winslow and Anna saw the signs for the ferry to Seattle. Suddenly the ferry itself appeared, brightly lit and ungainly at the end of the dock, then disappeared behind the trees as the car continued south on the island road.

"Garrett. Perhaps you should have let me off."

"It's raining, Anna."

"But I could just take the ferry back by myself."

"Don't be ridic—" He never finished the word because the car swayed abruptly as the front tire blew out. The car limped off the side of the road, the tire flop-flopping and Garrett swearing pungently. The rain washed over the metal roof of the car.

"I know what you're thinking, Anna. I didn't plan this."

She hid a grin in her hand. "I know you didn't."

"That's a relief. I'm not too good with mechanical objects. But we're in luck. I *have* changed a tire before. Ten years ago."

"Do you need help?"

"No point in us both getting wet. But thanks. I was sitting here entertaining the faint, fond hope that the rain would abate. But it has the appearance of wanting to continue until March. So here we go. Wish me luck."

And he was out of the car. Anna twisted around to see him through the back window as he popped open the trunk. She heard various heavy somethings bouncing around. She couldn't bear to sit there while he was struggling and got out.

"Get back in the car," he shouted.

"Let me help you. Chivalry in this weather is stupid."

He looked at her and handed her something heavy and metallic. "Hold this so it doesn't float away." Then he shouted "Aha!" in triumph and held out an elderly, rusty, black umbrella.

The umbrella had a tear and didn't quite reach the end of its ribs in a couple of places, but it kept the rain off the object of their attention. The whole business took four times longer than usual since neither of them was well versed in the art. One person stopped to ask if they needed help but by that time Garrett was letting the car down off the jack. They hurried back into the car and sat shivering and sputtering.

"Well, that was an experience I could have done without. Thanks for your help."

"Lord, I'm cold." She couldn't stop her teeth from chattering.

"Silly woman. You should have taken advantage of my stupid but chivalrous offer and stayed in the dry." He switched on the heater full blast. The windows immediately fogged. "Damn. Well, we'll be there in no time," he assured her as he opened his window to see out. "If the spare holds out."

"What do you mean 'if'?"

"Just a manner of speaking." After about a half mile they turned left sharply into a narrow, tree-lined lane. The car bumped and bucked along the wet and rutted road before coming to a halt by a small, angular wood-and-glass house.

"Stay here while I unlock the place and throw on the electric switch," she heard him say. She felt very cold as she huddled in her sodden clothes. She couldn't stop shivering. She tried to concentrate on taking deep breaths. Suddenly the porch light flooded the area with light. "Come on," he was urging her as he held the car door open.

She stumbled a little as he helped her onto the covered porch. "My feet," she said. "They're numb."

"Come on in. We'll get you warmed up."

She realized dimly that he was as soaked as she. She stood inside the door and worried about making water marks on the wide plank floors. The air in the house was cold and dank. Garrett disappeared and came back, pulling a dry shirt over his bare torso. "I'll get a fire started. Here, put this on." He handed her a thick terry-cloth robe and disappeared again into the main room.

The robe was ice-white and cold to the touch. The whole world was suddenly cold. Anna was trying to fit her arms into it and was still struggling when Garrett came back. He wrapped the robe around her like a cloak and lifted her easily into his arms, crushing her cheek against the dry warmth of his shoulder. He set her down on the stone hearth, where a fire was trying to come to life, and blew on the young flames.

She knew he was talking to her and she tried to listen, but she couldn't concentrate. He was holding her hands in his, chafing them. Then he was rubbing her arms. He called her name and she looked at him and tried to smile. She was all right, she knew. Just cold. She couldn't seem to get the words out.

He disappeared again and came back with a towel and a large glass of something. It tasted cold and hot all at the same time, and she knew she'd had some once before.

"... Clothes off."

She heard the words distinctly and focused on Garrett. "No," she said automatically and saw him shake his head and smile.

"Listen to me. We've got to get you out of these wet clothes and into dry ones. Now, lift your arms, Anna..."

Her sodden sweater left. Then her blouse was quickly unbuttoned and peeled from her. And instant later the big robe was back around her. But then he stood her up and undid her jeans. She protested, pushing at his hands. In vain. She couldn't feel her feet but she could see her shoes were soaked through. He took the shoes off, peeled off her socks and wrapped her feet in a towel. Then he put another towel over her head and squeezed at it gently.

She focused on him again. He was kneeling there in front of her, offering her another sip of brandy. It was brandy. She knew that now. He smiled at her. She could feel the warmth of the fire. "You're looking better. I'm going up to run you a hot bath. When you're back to room temperature we'll have dinner."

"How about you?"

"I'm fine. Worrying about you got me all warmed up."

Her legs and feet resisted it; they hated it. Her whole body shrieked at her, but she forced it down, down into the hot water. The pain dulled as the steam filled her nostrils, and what she felt then was the tingling awakening that was a prelude to real warmth. Immersed past her chin in the heavy heat, she sighed deeply: she was going to survive.

As her body warmed, her brain slowly began to function again. And her eyes snapped open. There was the robe, white and voluminous on the tile floor. And there was the brandy, golden in a cut-glass snifter. The bathroom was large, walled in rough cedar. Framed posters of musical instruments hung on the cedar. The faucets were brass and needed polishing.

"Should I call the Coast Guard?" a voice inquired from the other side of the door.

Startled, she jerked and splashed a quantity of water over the edge of the tub. "I'm fine," she blurted out in a too-high voice. Then the absurdity of it took over. She laughed. "I'm afraid there isn't room for the Coast Guard in here. Thanks just the same. I'll be out in a jiff."

"Anna?" his voice came again through the door.

"Yes?"

The door opened a crack and she drew herself into a ball. Some clothing dropped on the floor. "These won't fit, but at least they're dry and I warmed them by the fire. It's really roaring down there now."

"Thanks, Garrett."

He'd given her a roomy maroon sweatshirt and a pair of blue cotton drawstring pants, soft from many washings. As she slipped the sweatshirt over her head she breathed in his smell and caught her reflection in a smile. She made a face in reply and set about repairing the damage to her hair with the comb and brush she found in a drawer. She already knew the effort was hopeless. Her hair would kink and curl gaily into a zillion ringlets and that was all there was to it. She was deciding to give up the fight when smells from the kitchen filled her nostrils.

"Mmm," she announced from the door of the kitchen. It was a pullman with a brick floor and red cabinets, and Garrett was shaking something aromatic in an iron skillet.

"A little smoked salmon with cream and parmesan tossed about in al dente linguine. How does that sound?"

"Heavenly," she said sincerely.

He looked at her directly, the skillet aloft in his capable hand. "How are you?"

"Quite toasty, thanks."

He grinned and went back to shaking the contents of the pan. "That's good news. You were quite blue. Let's eat."

They took their plates into the main room and Anna got her first real look at it. While not large, its main features were striking: an entire stone wall that held the blazing hearth, two walls of windows reflecting the room back at itself, and the piano. It was quite unlike the sleek ebony grand in his Seattle house. This was an antique, heavy, ornate, carved walnut, solid as a century. The rest of the furniture, a couch, three chairs, a low table, was all serviceable, weekend-cottage sort of furniture: comfortable, dark, immortal. They ate dinner at the table, pulled in front of the fireplace.

"That's the second time you've saved my life."

"A slight exaggeration. Though why on earth you insisted on standing outside in all that rain, I'll never understand. Didn't you feel yourself getting chilled?"

"I'm kind of stubborn that way."

"No, really?"

"This is terrific," she said. "You are a fantastic cook."

"So I'm forgiven?"

"For what?"

"For luring you here. I half expected you to run away while I was buying this stuff at the store."

She remembered considering just that and flushed. "Garrett. Can't we just leave things the way they are?"

"No. I don't think so." His light gray irises surrounded deep black wells.

"You don't understand."

"That's not true. I do. I understand you're afraid. Of me. Or of yourself. I want to know why."

"It's the situation...."

"Damn the situation. Let me worry about the situation. We're both adults, Anna. Mature, reasonable adults. We can handle it. If anybody can, we can. But you won't even give it a chance. The instant something shifts and the feelings begin to surface, you close me out completely. You close yourself out, as well."

Her gaze dropped away even though she willed it not to. The embers burned white hot at the center of the log.

"Anna?"

"You're mistaken," was all she said.

"Not about my feelings for you." Then he was there next to her, kneeling, taking her face in his hands and slowly, slowly bringing his lips to hers. Gently at first. For the first time in what seemed like forever she tasted him again, the deep, sweet, fragrant saltiness of him, and hunger leaped deep within her. She gave to him without a thought, and he absorbed her gift, pressing her against him, responding to her response. He released her at last and watched her face intently.

His eyes smiled as he traced the line of her cheek with a gentle finger. "And I don't think I'm mistaken about your feelings for me."

Tears filled her eyes and threatened to spill over. "Please," she murmured. "I can't help what I feel. But I can't do what you want...."

He frowned. "Is there somebody else, Anna? Because if..."

"No," she said before she thought, and then wished she'd lied. She pulled away from him.

He stood up suddenly, thrust his hands into his pockets and strode across the room. "I'm so damned sick of pretending. Pretending what's there isn't there. Pretending what I feel doesn't matter or will go away." He turned and looked at her. "You seem to think I've set out to stalk you or something. When just the opposite is true, Anna. I didn't want this to happen. You'll remember I agreed with you and promised I wouldn't..." He stopped and sat down heavily on the bench again.

"I've tried to keep the distance there. But it hasn't worked. There are times when I just want to be with you. Talk to you. There are times when I feel so close to you...like today, this afternoon. Just talking. Just standing next to you. And playing music. This afternoon playing those sonatas was like nothing I've ever experienced before, Anna. And I know I want more than just that. I want you. All of you, Anna. I want to make love to you. I want..."

She put her hands over her ears. "Please stop this," she said loudly to drown him out. "I can't deal with this."

He said nothing. When she raised her head he was sitting on the piano bench near the window, his elbows resting on his thighs, his hands dangling, staring at the floor. She bit her lip and asked him, "Tell me, Garrett, what's the most important thing in your life."

His smile was odd when he lifted his head and said without hesitation, "Music. Of course."

"Music. Of course." She imitated his tone exactly and he frowned. "You didn't say women or sex or marriage or children. Or me, did you? You said, 'Music. Of course.'" Garrett watched her carefully. "Well," she continued in a stronger voice, "it's what I say, too. Music. Of course. It's my whole life. It always has been. If it weren't, I wouldn't even be here...with you...in this room." She gestured widely then huddled in her large clothes.

When she went on, her voice was lower. "Music. It's what I love most in the world. It's all I really care about," she added slowly, weighing every word. "I work at it and love it and hate it and think about it all the time. Everything I do centers around music. Everything I've ever done. And I don't like it when anything threatens to interfere with my music. Whether it's a cold or a late bus. Or somebody like you, who just wants and doesn't consider the cost or consequences to anyone else."

He stared at her for a moment. "You're not telling me anything I don't already know, Anna. We're both of us serious musicians. Dedicated musicians. The strangest animal there is. Insane by definition. I think that's part of our common bond. Yours and mine. We're a lot alike." She started to interrupt him, but he shook his head and went on. "Being a musician, however, doesn't preclude being human. Your violin doesn't have any affection for you."

"You're making fun of me."

"No. Far from it, Anna. I'm trying to tell you something important."

"You're trying to convince me to go to bed with you. Next you'll say that only another human being can show me affection. You'll probably call it love."

He winced and looked away. She felt a pinprick of triumph that she'd scored a wound. But it was followed by a wave of misery, a yearning to deny her words, to apologize. She pushed on in a hoarse voice. She had to convince him and herself. "I'm trying to tell you that I don't want what you're offering. I don't want anyone. I prefer being alone."

"You've never known anything else, have you?"

"That's not true."

"Then you wouldn't be so terrified of admitting that you . . ."

"Can you deny that you planned all along to bring me here? And wear me down and take me to bed?"

"What's that got to do with anything?"

"The fact that it's true just negates everything you're saying."

"God, Anna." He stood up and stalked to the window as a barrage of windy rain smashed against the glass. "You seem to need to cast me in the role of a rapist or a monster." He turned to her and spread his hands. "I'm just a man. A man you said you liked not so very many hours ago. As long as we talk about the music and the weather or the past, you like me. But when I try to talk about now, about my feelings, about your feelings, then I'm a villain. Yes, I wanted to bring you here. Just to be with you without all the clamor going on. Just to talk. At the end of a weekend during which we played glorious music, not as conductor and musician, but as equals.

"I hadn't really planned to seduce you, Anna. It's not really my style. I want to make love to you. I believe you feel something for me. I thought perhaps if we gave ourselves the chance, we could work it all out to our mutual satisfaction. But I won't ask again. And I'd never force you, Anna. So you needn't look at me like that with those huge brown eyes."

The faint bleat of a ferry penetrated the storm. Garrett glanced at his watch. "That's the last one till morning. We should probably have tried to make it." He covered his eyes for a moment. "God, I'm tired."

She'd won and she hated it. She wanted to go to him and put her arms around him, feel his around her and lose herself. It was crazy.

"Garrett?"

"Hmm?"

"I'll sleep on the couch."

"You can have my room."

"I'd be more comfortable here."

"I'm sure that's true," he replied.

"Garrett. I'm sorry that I've disappointed you."

"Forget it. You didn't. I mean, that's not what..."

"I appreciate your understanding. I think this is best."

"I don't really agree. But I'm giving it up. I draw the line at playing the fool. Or the villain."

"Are we still friends?"

"Oh, Anna. I'll be anything you want me to be. Friend. Lover. Even brother. Boss. Monster." He lifted his lip and snarled. "Vampire, maybe?"

She laughed.

"Thank God. I thought you were going to die of seriousness. And don't worry about me. Nobody ever died of what I'm suffering from."

He brought her a pillow and a sheet and two blankets. As he turned to leave again, he hesitated and then faced her, a faint smile in place. "I just want you to know that if you should change your mind about all this, I'd be happy to reopen negotiations."

"You'll be the first to know. Sleep well, Garrett."

"Don't bet on it."

And she was alone.

Chapter Eight

Her nose was buried in the cedary smell of the rough wool blanket, and when she opened her eyes she was looking into dimly glowing coals. She knew instantly where she was, and she knew she'd only been asleep a short while. She'd watched that same fire die to coals long after Garrett had gone up to bed and the sounds of his restlessness had ceased.

What had awakened her? She listened, dimly convinced it had been a tiny noise, its echo still in her brain. There was only silence now. She was alone. She stretched and changed positions on the couch, huddling into her blankets, willing her eyes to shut, her brain to go back to sleep before it began to work again.

But it was too late. She was already remembering. She might never have slept at all. Again she was reliving the entire day and evening, as she had already a hundred times. Already she'd thought over each word, measured each response and come up with the same inevitable conclusion: she was right. She was absolutely right. But now as before, this sure knowledge came with no sense of joy, no feeling of satisfaction, no surge of elation. She felt instead an overwhelming desolation, a feeling of profound loss, an oppressive sadness. That was what had pervaded her brief sleep and was persisting now that she was awake again. Forcing her to go over it again and again.

There it was. The noise. A small noise, but she knew it was what had awakened her. It came from the kitchen. Maybe it was a mouse, used to having the house to himself, searching for crumbs. A larger intruder? Then she heard liquid pouring into a glass and sat up. Garrett. There in the next room.

Her imagination made the brief journey: she saw herself getting up and going to him. It would be over, then, all the struggle, the endless doubt, the charade of pretending. He was tired of pretending, he'd said. Well, so was she. He wanted her, he'd said. He'd shown her a little of what it would be like to be wanted, to be with someone instead of forever alone. Maybe it was time to take the risk. To be foolish this once, instead of wise. To be loved, however briefly.

In the space of a single breath, Anna had decided. And she didn't give herself time to think again. She slipped from under the blanket, clad only in his dark red sweatshirt that came down to her thighs. Her bare feet made no noise on the wide planking.

He was putting the brandy bottle away over the sink, shutting the cabinet door carefully, noiselessly.

In the darkness she could see he had on the white robe he'd lent her earlier. His hair was tousled, boyish-looking from the back. He turned and saw her, and for an instant neither of them moved.

"Anna?"

"I couldn't sleep, either."

"Do you want some brandy?" His voice was tight, held in.

"No."

Anna took the first step and knew there was no going back. The small room was charged, heavy, airless. "Garrett. You're going to have to help me. I don't know the words. I don't know how to ask."

There was a silence that lasted a single heartbeat. "Come here," he whispered.

As if in a dream she took three more steps and she was so close she could feel his heat. Her eyes rested in his; they were all she could see, all she ever wanted to see. Very gently he took her face in his long hands, his fingers delving deeply into her hair, his thumbs softly stroking the angle of her jaw, his eyes searching hers, seeking answers.

She leaned toward him very slightly and felt his fingers tighten and heard his breath catch in his throat. He whispered her name once before he claimed her mouth. Her lips parted and she gave him her answer.

Anna lost consciousness of everything that wasn't Garrett. His strong arms and hands, his warm smell, his mouth and tongue and teeth were all that existed, all that had ever existed. She couldn't get enough of him. Desire she'd never imagined took hold of her and she gave herself up to it completely.

When her breath was gone, her reason obliterated, she felt his hands pushing gently on her shoulders as he drew back from her. She leaned toward him again, seeking him blindly, but he held her away. "Anna." She looked up into his eyes. The most astonishing eyes she'd ever looked into. Worlds. He stroked her face gently, asking her, "Are you sure? Are you awake?"

She placed her finger against his mouth and whispered, "Yes. Yes." There was no fear. She was beyond any emotion she could name. She was in a completely new country where there were no boundaries, no limits to what she might do.

She put her arms around his neck and as she reached to kiss him again he lifted her easily in his arms and carried her up to his room. A single bedside lamp shed a soft light over the chaos of the bed. Without a word he set her on her feet, then framed her face gently, asking once more, silently.

In answer, she pushed at the bulky robe, and he dropped his arms so that it could fall to the floor. Anna's hands found the warm firm muscles of his back and arms, delighting in the feel of his warm skin, marveling at the softness and the strength of him, the gentleness and the power. She felt him tremble at her touch as she kissed the hollow of his shoulder.

He lifted her head to meet her in another kiss as his hands ran on thrilling journeys beneath her loose shirt. Anna arched her body as her senses soared. Then the sweatshirt was gone, pulled off over her head, and there were no more barriers between them. Nakedness against nakedness. This was new. So deliciously new that it took her breath away.

Gently he took her to the bed and laid her back in its softness. Then she felt him pull away and she opened her eyes to see him gazing at her. She should have felt shy and was amazed that she didn't. She lay there basking in his look, feeling desired, utterly desirable as his gaze traveled over her and came lazily back to hers.

"You're beautiful," he whispered. "Exquisite."

"So are you."

His hands and mouth were gentle and demanding and everywhere at once. When his mouth found her breast, Anna felt the last shreds of her reason scatter. Her hands seemed to develop a will of their own. They learned the shape of his muscles, the way his limbs joined, the way the hair swirled at his chest and belly, where his skin was soft as a child's. They learned how to make him tremble. They learned how to make him moan and gasp.

She heard her name whispered again and again, and then she was beneath his body, covered with his warmth, being asked to give now what she'd never given anyone before. And she wanted what he wanted. She wrapped her arms around his neck and clung tightly as she pressed up against him, arching, opening to him.

He entered her with a single thrust. She gasped at the suddenness, at the brief pain, and felt his whole body tighten and his head lift. The pain was gone before she could name it. But he didn't move. For an endless moment, their bodies were locked together in absolute stillness. Then he murmured her name softly and kissed her with such tenderness that tears filled her eyes.

Very slowly, very gently he began to move inside her, as his hands caressed her, soothed her, excited her. The momentary pain was forgotten completely as her body tuned to his. He kissed a trail down her neck and again found her breast, where he tasted and suckled and teased. Anna's body unleashed itself. She began to move against him, responding instinctively, moving with him in rhythm and counterrhythm in an ever-increasing tempo. She heard him cry out hoarsely and felt the joy of his release as her own universe exploded into brilliant shards of pure sensation.

Slowly she climbed and circled into consciousness. She felt so warm. Complete. Contented. She snuggled into the warmth of the body cradling her own and wished she could purr. A hand stroked her head and hair and she sighed.

Her own name poured around her as he whispered and stroked. His body shifted and she opened her eyes to find she was looking into his. He'd taken his weight off her and was leaning on an elbow, holding her, watching her.

"Hello." He smiled and touched her cheek.

"Hi."

For several moments he simply looked at her, his eyes full of emotion and wonder. His fingers curled her hair behind her ears and traced the line of her jaw. She wanted it to go on and on. Then his eyes changed, darkened, and his voice sounded blurry. "Why didn't you tell me, Anna?"

She hid her face against his shoulder. "I don't know," she murmured. "I guess I didn't know how. And then it didn't really matter anymore."

She felt his chin rubbing against her head as his arm tightened around her. "I hurt you."

"No. Not really."

"If only I'd known...if you'd only told me, I could have been gentler."

"You were gentle, Garrett."

"You amaze me. After trying to convince you I wasn't a monster, I come on like Attila the Hun."

She laughed at him. "Not quite." She wiggled up so she could kiss his mouth. "It's all right. I'm all right."

He tucked his head so he could look at her. "I couldn't believe it was happening. I kept thinking it was a dream."

"Me, too."

He lay back with a sigh and gathered her into his arms. Her head nestled into his shoulder, her arm draped over his chest, and their legs tangled together under the sheets. She felt she'd come to a place she'd been looking for all her life.

"Comfortable?" he asked.

"Mmm. Wonderful." She snuggled closer.

"You are. Incredible."

"Mmm."

"Sleepy?"

Anna didn't answer that time. She was asleep.

She didn't know he'd left; she only knew she was alone in the big bed. Alone and listening to Brahms and smelling coffee. Sunlight flooded the bed from the skylight overhead. And Garrett was downstairs playing Brahms. Late Brahms. His last works for solo piano: complex, lyrical, passionate. Anna listened and let the music pull her inside of it, until she could hear

Garrett's touch and feel it. Her whole body glowed and hummed with him. She smiled and stretched, lay back in the disordered bed and tried to want him less. Which only made her want him more.

A final chord died away and then there was silence below. She watched the doorway, expecting him. A minute passed and she heard nothing. She continued to watch, hoping he would come. Another minute. A very long minute. What was he doing? Would he come to her now? As if in answer to her unspoken questions, the music began again.

Fighting down her disappointment, she tried to listen to it. She didn't recognize it. She rejected every composer that ran through her brain. Snatches and pieces of it seemed familiar, but the whole blended into something else she couldn't identify. She was sitting up, trying to sort it out, getting frustrated, then angry. She was alone. Alone when it was the last thing she wanted.

The music filled the house, which seemed too small to contain the sounds. When he hammered the bass, the very rafters seemed to shake. Anna searched the floor and pulled on the only article of clothing that came to hand, the maroon sweatshirt. Her own clothes were scattered about downstairs. She opened the door of the room, then crept down the steps.

From the doorway she saw him in half profile. He was leaning back slightly, his eyes closed, and the music poured from his hands. Complicated, rhythmic, richly harmonic, the music wasn't what Anna wanted to hear. It taunted her. It told her that he'd forgotten her completely, that he'd turned back to his first, his truest love: his music, his piano. For a moment she stood bereft, realizing for the first time what real loneliness was. How naive she'd been to think she had known it before.

The warm glow she'd felt on waking was gone now and she shivered. The maddening music clashed and clanged around her ears. She shut it out and entered the room, intent on retrieving her clothes, clothing her nakedness, erasing the night.

The sounds ceased.

"Anna."

"Sorry to disturb you," she said primly. "I thought I'd better get dressed, you know."

He'd half risen, but now he slowly sat again. "Good morning," he said, and his voice seemed tentative.

She hunched into the big shirt as she grabbed at her clothes, dried now and stiff where they'd been spread on the stone hearth. In reply to his greeting she gave him a small, brief smile.

"Are you all right, Anna?"

"Yes. I'm fine, thank you."

He stood up now and started for her, but she sidestepped him and kept out of range. "Anna..." he began again.

"Just don't, Garrett. Don't say anything. I'm just going to take a shower and get dressed. I'm fine." She glanced up and saw hurt and confusion dash across his face before it settled into a troubled frown.

"I woke up early," he was saying, "and I knew if I stayed with you, I'd never want to leave."

She might not have heard him. "Do I smell coffee?"

"Anna..."

"I'll be down in a minute." She knew she'd run from the room. But it didn't matter.

The shower helped. She scrubbed herself hard, eradicating his scent, waking up her skin, washing away the night. She finished with icy water and put on her scratchy clothes and looked in the mirror.

Her hair was in riotous disorder. She attacked it with a brush and gathered it into a pony tail at the base of her neck. Her eyes stared back at her, huge and brown. Her face was flushed, her lips still swollen from the night. This, she knew, was the cold light of day. She'd acted on impulse and now came the payoff. She felt tears well up and she blinked them back, straightening her spine, practicing a carefree smile. Don't make a fool of yourself, she warned her reflection.

He was standing on the deck outside the kitchen when she came down. His back was to her, his hands were on his hips and he was staring down through the trees at the water. Sunshine dappled the window.

She found the coffee and was pouring herself a large red cupful when she saw the pad under the wall phone. In a tiny, tidy script it read, *Monday. 11:30—Tyler, 12:30—lunch w/NPR (Collins), 4:12—Pam's plane (Fl #332), 7:30 reh.*

She turned to face him as he entered the kitchen. "It's Monday," she announced.

"I know," he replied and grimaced. "All day. It was the second thing I thought of when my eyes opened this morning. If I hadn't remembered, I'd still be involved with the first thing. You." Now his smile warmed his eyes.

"You should have waked me."

"I did." He shrugged in the direction of the piano. "The music. My own special alarm clock."

"Oh." She turned away and took a sip of the coffee. "Mmm," she said. "This is good. By the way, what was it? I knew the Brahms, but not the other." By the time she'd turned back, she felt as if she knew the script. She sounded casual, normal, uninvolved. Surely this was the way real adults acted.

He was looking at her curiously. "It was Downing, opus eleventy-five or so. I lose track. It came out of my head. Or my heart."

Her chuckle went awry. "I was going crazy trying to identify it."

"If you listened to it, you heard a lot. A lot more than I can say right now."

"I guess I didn't. I mean I was just trying to..."

"Pin it down, I know." He folded his arms and rocked back on his heels. "Well. It doesn't matter. It's gone. That's music at best. Here one moment, gone the next. What do the philosophers say? Organized sound enclosed by time? Something like that."

She couldn't think of anything to say and looked away.

"Well. Time marches on." He began to wash his mug out. "I'm afraid we have to catch a ferry in forty-five minutes. I tried to cancel my first appointment, but didn't get very far. The man involved helped keep the orchestra afloat one entire bleak season, so I can't really afford to alienate him."

The words bubbled out unbidden. "We should have gone back last night."

She felt the slow weight and heat of his eyes. "You mean that, don't you?"

"With all my heart." Their eyes locked.

"I'm sorry, Anna," he said softly, in the voice she remembered from the night before. "This wasn't how I planned it."

"So you did plan it."

He shook his head. "I don't mean last night. That was..."

"Oh, right. I was the one who came to you. You couldn't have counted on that."

"Anna." He moved to her and tried to touch her face, but she pulled away so he had to drop his hand. "Last night meant more to me than I can say. What you did was wonderful. I was touched. I am. Touched. Moved. There aren't any words..." He paused. "I meant just now that today, the morning after, should be different from this. We shouldn't have to go anywhere. I want it to be perfect for you. Perfect. Idyllic." He gestured outside. "The sun's shining. You should have strawberries and cream for breakfast. We should go for a sail. Make love again." Again a pause. "Only this time..."

"What?"

"This time I'd move slowly. And I'd... Oh, dammit, Anna. I'm grateful for what you gave me. But I..."

"But you're not interested in virgins, is that it?"

"Don't put words in my mouth. I'm concerned about you. You, Anna. I feel responsible. Or rather, damned irresponsible." He ran his hand through his hair. "I guess I should have known. Should have been prepared. But as it is, you weren't protected, were you?"

She shrugged and wished she could disappear. "No. But it's all right."

He looked away. "I guess I'm used to more experienced women who..." His voice ground to a halt and he glanced at her.

"I'll take care of myself. You don't have to feel responsible. It was my fault. Chalk it up to momentary insanity. If we're going, we'd better get going. I mean..."

He caught her by the wrist as she tried to leave. "Don't do this."

"Please let me go."

"Not until you look at me."

She glared at him. "There. Now let me go."

"What happened last night wasn't insane. It was beautiful. It was the most beautiful thing that's ever happened to me. I've never..."

"Spare me the lines, Garrett. I don't want to listen to them."

He winced as if she'd hit him. But she got her hand back. "We're going to miss the ferry."

"To hell with the ferry."

"It's just as well. Even if we'd spent the day together, we'd still have to go back sooner or later. Go back to business as usual. And the longer we stayed, thc hardcr it would bc to go back to the real world. The harder it would be to know how to act."

"What do you mean?"

"Well, how do you want me to behave? At rehearsal tonight, for instance." He just looked at her, so she filled in the blank. "Like nothing happened, right?"

"Why are you doing this?"

"Doing what?"

"Making this into something awful?"

"Because it never should have happened."

He looked at her. "But it did, Anna. We can't change that now."

"But we have to pretend it didn't."

"I didn't say that."

"But it's true. We have to treat each other the same way as before, as if nothing had happened. The pretending isn't going to stop. Part of me knew that all along. I just forgot it for a minute last night."

He was silent in the car. On the ferry he bought a newspaper and gave her a section. They sat and read over bad coffee in foam cups and stale doughnuts on napkins. Sitting across the little table like an old married couple, she thought. Nothing to say after all these years. After all these hours. She couldn't wait to get to Seattle. She wanted to be alone in her own house and work it out, pound and shape the past day and night into something she could live with.

In front of her house he opened the car door for her and even carried her duffel bag and violin, even though she said she could handle them. He stood there while she unlocked her door and set her violin and bag inside. "Anna. This isn't the end of it."

"It should be."

"We just both have some thinking to do."

"You're going to be late for your appointment."

He looked exasperated. "Call me if you need a ride to rehearsal."

"I'll manage." She gave him a grin that felt like a mask. "I'm a big girl now. I might even buy a car. You never know."

He seemed to hesitate, as if he were trying to say something else. Then he glanced at his watch and exhaled impatiently. "I'll see you tonight then." He turned to go, then turned back, his face a study in contradictory emotions. "I wish, Anna, that. . . ." He stopped and swallowed. "Well, it's not going to be an easy week."

"It never is."

"I mean I won't have any time to. . ."

"Just leave it, Garrett. I understand."

"That's good," he said, nodding at her. Then he shook his head angrily as hurt settled into his eyes. "Because I don't." His kiss brushed gently just to the east of her mouth. "Take care, Anna. I'll see you tonight."

She didn't watch him leave. She went inside and shut the door and leaned against it, listening. She couldn't hear his footsteps, but she heard the gate creak, then his car door open and slam, then the engine leap into life. And she was alone.

It would have been comforting to succumb to self-pity and sit and cry her eyes out. But one look at her calendar convinced Anna that she didn't have time for that luxury. Between that afternoon and the following Sunday afternoon she was playing in four concerts and nine rehearsals. Her first rehearsal was with the quartet at two that afternoon. She had never felt so grateful for a busy schedule. With any luck, there would be no time for thinking.

It wasn't until she saw Tom and Charlotte and Clark looking up at her as she entered the room that she realized it had been less than forty-eight hours since they'd played together. The quintets with Garrett. The feeling of triumph and accomplishment they'd all shared as the applause broke over them. It seemed so far away, as if it had happened a century ago.

She hurried in and began to unpack her instrument. "Sorry I'm late. The bus couldn't seem to get out of second. One of these days when I have a few hours to put together, I'm going car shopping. Anyone want to help?"

"I'll volunteer," said Tom. "Just say when."

"I'll have to check with my appointment secretary."

"How did Sunday go?" Charlotte asked as Anna settled into her chair.

"Oh, fine. About one-hundred folks in their Sunday best. And this magnificent thunderstorm. It was great. It came crashing down in the middle of the softest part of the Schubert."

"And the music" Tom prompted. "How'd that go?"

"I think it sounded all right," she admitted offhandedly. "Garrett's a good accompanist." She'd even said his name. She frowned at the music in front of her. "Let's start on the Beethoven," she said. "It's the one that hasn't quite come together and Wednesday is nearly here."

At 7:20 Anna was sorting through the music on her stand as the musicians bustled into their seats, discussing the weather and the coming weekend. The orchestra would be playing a special outdoor Fourth of July concert on Saturday evening in the band shell at Volunteer Park. All American music: Ives, Copland, Barber, Bernstein.

Her stand partner seated himself and got busy rosining his bow. "Hello, Hal."

"Anna," he replied without looking at her. She found herself suddenly wishing he were concertmaster. He was fifty-five and competent. He combed his thinning black hair so carefully over his bald head. He was never late. He played in tune, usually. He wasn't involved with the conductor.

"We've got our work cut out for us this week," she said pleasantly, feeling a wave of compassion for the man. She could see where he'd cut himself shaving before rehearsal.

"We played the same concert last year." He coughed. "Nearly the same," he amended.

"Good. Then you can tell me how he wants this."

His ragged eyebrows lifted as he looked at her in surprise. "The Barber?"

"Uh-huh. *'Knoxville, 1915.'* I can tell it's a lovely song, but I've never played it. I don't think I've even ever heard it. Who's singing it?"

"The conductor's ex."

"Who?"

"Sara Santini. She and Downing were married for a minute or two a couple of years back. In fact, she sang this last year. Made such a hit they hired her to come back and do it again."

Sara. "I thought she lived in Chicago," Anna murmured because she couldn't think of anything else to say.

"Well, she's coming back to sing this. Who knows? Maybe they like to get together now and then. Ours is not to wonder." His pale blue eyes focused suddenly beyond her. "Of course, it may get complicated." She followed the direction of his look and saw Garrett coming through a door of the auditorium with a tall blonde. "Old girl friend, that one," Hal was saying. "This could be interesting."

"Is her name Pam?" Anna heard herself asking. The list had read "Pam's plane." She'd managed to forget it until now.

"Pamela Winter or something like that. God, I can't keep track of his women. But I remember her face."

She watched Garrett talking to the woman and felt something die inside. Dimly she heard Hal speaking. "I wanted to tell you. I heard the quintets the other night, Anna. It was a good piece of work. I wanted you to know that."

"Thank you." She looked at him, her amazement at his unexpected praise slightly stifled by her confusion at what was going on in the auditorium.

He lowered his voice and she had to lean a bit to hear him. "When I first got a look at you, I figured Downing had hired you with his bed in mind. I know he gave you a hard time at first, but I figured it was an act. To cover up what was going on on the side. But I guess I was wrong. You've proved yourself. And I owe you an apology."

She leaned back but was saved from articulating a response by Garrett's saying, "People, let's get started. We've got an audience tonight. And she's taking notes. Pamela!" he called to the woman, and she approached the stage. A stunning, tall woman with a blond pageboy and a wide-shouldered, peach-tone linen suit, flawless makeup, perfect bones and a model's smile.

Anna heard what Garrett said without looking up again. "This is Pamela Frost, for those of you who have short memories or haven't been here long. Pam used to be on the orchestra board, then moved to L.A. to learn the ways of the recording industry. She'll be here through Friday, going to concerts and dropping in on rehearsals. And not just because she loves music. She's up here to see if we can negotiate a record contract."

He waited while the news sank in. Anna was wondering where Pamela was staying as Garrett continued. "A well-timed record could make a large difference to our future as an orchestra. I hope I don't have to tell you that. So play beautifully, children, and convince her that she's not wasting her time. Then she can go back and convince her boss that we're a good investment. Anna." She looked up, startled at being addressed. "Get the orchestra ready, please."

In the instant that followed, Anna's thoughts traveled at lightning speed. She took in Garrett and his smile, his open-necked white shirt and unexpected red suspenders, the pleated seersucker slacks. He looked gorgeous, charming, suave, sophisticated. She took in Pam as she walked gracefully back to her seat in the front row. She ran through the past two days of her life and felt like hitting Garrett over the head with her violin. And leaving. Just walking out. But the instant passed. And instead she stood up and faced the musicians. She smiled at the oboist and asked her for an A and, section by section, she tuned the orchestra.

Chapter Nine

On Thursday Anna had lunch with Pamela Frost in a restaurant overlooking the Pike Place Market. The day was sunny, the Brazilian chicken perfectly complemented by rice pilaf and a tangy salad. The sun glanced through Anna's glass of sparkling water and decorated her plate with rainbows.

"I'm worried about him," Pamela was saying, and she was talking about Garrett. The entire conversation had centered on Garrett almost from the moment they'd sat down, and Anna had discovered that she didn't have to contribute. Pamela liked to talk, and she particularly liked to talk about Garrett.

Only three days had gone by. It had seemed like an eternity to Anna. Muffling unfamiliar and agonizing twinges of jealousy in silence and denial, she had focused intently on her work. She had almost succeeded in making Sunday night's fit of passion into something that had never happened. Almost. She could watch Pamela and Garrett together almost with indifference. Almost. On the edge of rage on several occasions, she had been able to step back, take a cold look at herself and lodge the blame for her anger firmly on her own shoulders. She simply should have known better.

"I'm really worried about him," Pamela repeated. "I've never seen him this wound up. He's like a wire that's stretched too thin. He's barely eating or sleeping. I watch him pick at his food and I lie there listening to him pace the floor, not knowing whether to get up or not. I told him I was moving to a hotel today and he said he didn't blame me."

Anna tried to digest this information behind an expression she hoped masked everything she felt. She had tried not to think about Garrett and Pamela sharing his room. Now the evidence was in. The food in her mouth lost its taste; her throat closed up; she had to use all her energy just to swallow.

How could he? How could he have made love to her and then...she tried to shut it out and concentrate on what Pamela was saying. After all, it wasn't Pamela's fault. It was *her* fault. She'd been a fool. But it wouldn't happen again. She'd already managed the last three days pretty well. She'd tried to avoid seeing Garrett alone, and she'd succeeded, with one devastating exception.

They had had a Tuesday morning rehearsal scheduled for violin/piano sonatas. Pamela was planning to sit in, so Anna had arrived early, hoping to be ready to begin when they arrived. Instead she found Garrett sitting alone at the keyboard.

She steeled herself against the wave of confused emotions that threatened her balance and sent him what she hoped was an airy, impersonal "good morning" as she crossed the room to set down her instrument. When he didn't answer she was forced to look at him. His eyes were somber and smudged in an unusually pale face. His hair was disheveled. He looked like a man who'd missed a night's sleep as well as breakfast. She resisted the urge to ask him if he was all right. It crossed her mind that he might at least have made an attempt to look rested and innocent, not spent and bedraggled.

"Where's Pamela?" she asked brightly, determined to be normal, though she would have been at a loss to define the term.

"She'll be here in a few minutes. I was hoping you'd come a bit early. I was hoping we could have a little time together." He stood up as he spoke but Anna stayed where she was.

"I think we need the time we have to work, Garrett," Anna replied evenly, proud of the smooth way her brain was working. "I'm pretty shaky on the Haydn."

"I just want to talk to you, Anna," he said in a low, husky voice.

"If you come any closer, I'm gone, Garrett. I'm out of here." She watched him for a moment. "You're incredible," she said finally, when she found the right word. "You're capable of anything, aren't you?"

He searched her face. "Am I?" he said softly.

"Well, you know better than I. All I know is that I want to play music."

"I'm afraid I want more than that."

She blinked at him and pressed her lips together. "I don't want to have this conversation. Please leave me a little self-respect, Garrett. That's all I ask. Now I'm going to tune this violin and start to play. If you want to play along, fine."

He'd drawn breath to answer, but Pamela had popped into the room, much to Anna's profound relief.

"At first I thought it was the Festival that was bothering him," Pamela was going on. "But from what I've seen, it seems to be going well. The rehearsal Monday was certainly promising. And, Anna, last night was marvelous. Simply terrific."

"Thank you." The new Northwest Symphony Quartet had made its debut the previous evening in the covered courtyard of the Seattle Art Museum with a program of Beethoven, Dvořák and Shostakovich. The four musicians had emerged triumphant and glowing with accomplishment. Garrett and Pamela had been part of the standing-room-only audience. Afterward, Garrett's praise had been a smile, a slow shake of his head and the words "Well played."

"And I know that Garrett was very pleased with the quartet. He talked my ear off until after midnight. He especially talked about you."

"That must have been pretty exciting for you," Anna managed to say.

Pamela sipped her white wine. "Honestly, I couldn't believe it when he hired you. I ranted and raved for years on the orchestra board about hiring more women and minorities. They all looked like penguins, all these stuffy men in their black suits. When he phoned to say he'd hired you as concertmaster I was beside myself."

"I think he regretted it at first."

"No," Pamela contradicted as she frowned at the avocado slice she'd pierced with her fork. "He probably gave you that impression. Big mistake to take him personally sometimes. Oh, I think he thinks you're still pretty green, but he really is impressed with your musicianship. He thinks you'll go far. He just hopes you don't go too far too soon. He wants you to stick around for a while."

"Did he say that?"

"Maybe not in so many words."

"You've known him for a long time?"

"About eight years. I left Seattle two years ago. Horrendous divorce. Garrett was the only reason I lived through it. He listened to me rant and rave by the hour, even took my kids to the zoo one afternoon when I was afraid I was going to strangle both of them. He doesn't look like the kid type, but he's great with them. Treats them like miniature adults. Lots of respect. Anyway, he's a very good friend. Which is why I'm so damned worried about him."

The tiny frown line between her perfect eyebrows was the only flaw on Pamela Frost's face. Her makeup was invisible, her hair smooth as silk. Her teeth were straight out of a toothpaste ad. Her posture was a ballet dancer's. She fascinated Anna, whose interest in clothes didn't go beyond practicality and comfort, whose makeup often went forgotten, whose posture was frequently dictated by the sore neck and back of a violinist. And Pamela fascinated Anna, despite everything, because she seemed to know and understand Garrett Downing intimately.

Anna searched for something comforting to say to Garrett's concerned friend that wouldn't compromise the tiny past she herself had shared with him and wished she could forget. "I really do think it's probably nerves. Or maybe he's coming down with something," she suggested somewhat lamely.

"Yeah," countered Pamela. "And I think its name is Sara Santini. Some virus."

"I beg your pardon?"

"You *do* know who the soloist this weekend is, don't you?"

"For the Fourth of July concert? Oh. Yes, of course."

"Yup," nodded Pamela, "the former Mrs. Downing, though she was never that. Always Miss Santini, that one. God, what a disaster. I never understood it. I think she bewitched him. Voodoo or something."

"I don't know anything about it," murmured Anna. "I guess I never thought it was any of my business."

Pamela plowed on. "Garrett went to the Spoleto festival in Italy two summers ago to conduct. He met her, and I guess they set the whole place on fire. I mean really hot. She came back with him and within three months they were married. Then, ka-boom!—it was over by the following summer. Last year. Lord, how time flies. Personally I think it was over about the time it started. That sort of grand passion usually is."

Anna tried to agree in her heart and struggled to change the direction of the conversation. "So she's Italian."

"By heritage. Actually, I think she's from Brooklyn. Or Queens. She's absolutely beautiful, has a terrific voice, but she's the kind of woman you'd like to ban, you know?"

Anna didn't know and said nothing. Something Garrett had said Monday morning came back: it would be a difficult week, he'd said. That had to be the understatement of all times. He was faced with juggling an old flame, who was a potential business asset, an ex-wife, who was a featured soloist, and a brand-new lover, whose presence he couldn't avoid. A lesser man would probably have already left the country. Instead he was...well, juggling. And through Anna's confusion, resentment, anger, jealousy, an astonishing sentiment emerged: Poor Garrett.

"She sang last year, you know," Pamela was saying.

"Yes. So I understood."

"Just as things were dissolving, I mean marriage-wise. I wasn't here. But Garrett called me. He'd call sometimes and then not be able to say anything. He'd just ask about my life, ask me to talk, just say anything. But when I'd want to know what was wrong, he'd just say, 'Nothing.' I knew she was leaving him. I knew he was terribly unhappy. It made me so sad. I asked him if he wanted me to come up. He'd been such a rock during all my mess. But he said no. He said he was working hard. Practicing the piano six hours a day. Running a lot. I wish he'd told Sara not to come back. I don't see why he's putting himself through this."

Anna's mind was whirling. It took all of her presence of mind to reply calmly, "Perhaps he feels he can deal with it now. With her. He seems like a very strong person to me."

Pamela took a sip of wine and smiled wisely. "He's a marshmallow, Anna. Inside, I mean. Underneath that lean and mean exterior he's as vulnerable as a boy. It's part of his charm. When you get to know him, I mean."

"Well," said Anna, "you know him better than I."

Pamela studied her companion. "Do I detect something here?"

"I beg your pardon?"

"I don't know. Just for a second I thought I detected something in your voice. Something that told me that perhaps you've looked at Garrett as something other than your conductor."

Very carefully Anna looked at her. This was very strange. "I don't know what you mean."

The other woman smiled. "I'm not accusing you of anything, Anna. I was just a little surprised. I don't believe I've ever met anybody as, I don't know, as otherworldly as you. You're so focused. Music, music, music, you know. Like Garrett. But more so, though I'd never thought that possible. Like you have no use for the real world or anyone in it. Like I really didn't think you'd have lunch with me today."

"I wondered why you asked me."

"I know. You have no idea how fascinating you are. You're beautiful, you know. And very intelligent. And you have this serene aura that I feel masks an incredible amount of energy, and probably turmoil. It all comes out when you play. But the rest of the time you seem completely in control.''

Anna felt acutely uncomfortable under Pamela's steady blue gaze. ''Do you often analyze the people you're having lunch with?''

''Ow. Was that what I was doing? I didn't mean to offend you. I guess you interest me. By what you've accomplished. By who you are. And, I don't deny it, by what Garrett has told me about you. I think he . . . well, I shouldn't say this. But whenever I say that, I usually just go ahead. Damn the torpedoes. I think he'd like to get to know you better. And not as a musician. Something in his eyes when he talks about you.''

''Listen, I really don't . . .''

''Oh, I know. I'm out of line. Besides there's the situation. Awful situation. But you can't deny you're attracted to him?''

''I'm just not sure what that has to do with anything.''

''Oh, God. I've stuck my foot in it. I'm sorry. Forget everything I've said. Let's talk about the weather or something.''

Anna didn't see Garrett or Pamela again until Friday night, and when Garrett climbed on the podium for Friday's rehearsal, Anna received a jolt. He was very pale and his eyes were feverishly bright. His first words were inaudible. He coughed, clearing his throat and tried again in vain to make himself heard. Then he impatiently motioned to Anna to come up to him. ''Laryngitis,'' he whispered in her ear. ''Tell them, please, to get out the Bernstein. Ives next. Then Copland. We'll do the Barber last." He raised his eyebrows significantly. "I know that's not the order, Anna, but Miss Santini has been detained."

Anna spoke his words aloud to the orchestra, carefully including the nature of his illness and the part about Miss Santini. During the rehearsal, whenever he had something to say, he looked at Anna and she rose to go to him, listen and translate his hoarse whispers. During a break after the Ives, he beckoned to her again. "Thanks for your help," he whispered.

"You should probably be in bed," she whispered back.

"Funny how whispers beget whispers."

"Well, you should be," she repeated in her normal voice.

"I sound worse than I feel. Honestly. My throat isn't even sore."

"You look feverish."

"Do I?"

She looked around but they were in relative privacy. "What's keeping Miss Santini?"

"I am. I mean I asked her to come late. Last in rehearsal, first in the concert. I may be feverish, but I'm not stupid." He launched into a painful coughing fit that made Anna wince. He waved her off and when the attack had abated he climbed onto the podium and tapped for attention.

The detained lady made her entrance precisely as the Copland was winding up. Sara Santini obviously knew a lot about entrances. She burst onto the stage dressed in scarlet-and-black silk with a scarf braided around her head and a frown marring her otherwise beautifully dramatic features. She might have been the photographic negative of Pamela Frost: raven hair, dark eyes, olive skin. She was barely five four, full figured and fiercely intense.

Garrett stepped off his podium and, ever the gentleman, kissed her hand while murmuring something that Anna couldn't catch. Whatever it was brought a smile to Sara's face, and when she smiled she was absolutely ravishing.

The orchestra rehearsal had gone smoothly up to that point. Sara's song began well. A mezzo-soprano, her voice was stunning—rich, mature, flawless. The orchestra backed her up tactfully, Anna felt, and Garrett obviously knew his music and his artist well. But the gorgeous voice stopped abruptly after a slight bobble in a tricky measure.

"So what's this?" Sara Santini hissed at the conductor with her black eyes raging. The orchestra ground to a halt and Garrett looked at his soloist. "I said, what are you trying to do?"

He cleared his throat and made an effort to vocalize his words. "Let's take it again."

Sara Santini didn't like it. After the fifth try she marched off the stage, gesturing and talking loudly. Garrett and most of the orchestra stared after her, whereupon he turned back to his musicians and shrugged, lifted his baton and started the music without the singer. Fifteen seconds later Sara stomped back onto the stage. The music ceased. She glared sideways at the man to whom she had been married for ten months. "Oh, just start again. Just keep them quiet, will you? God, what an outfit." Anna watched Garrett's face as he heard Sara's orders; it was drained of all color, and the muscles of his jaw knotted briefly then relaxed. Without comment or gesture he turned from the woman and tapped his baton.

The concert went well, all things considered. The night was hot and still, forcing the orchestra into shirtsleeves before the scantily dressed crowd in Volunteer Park. Garrett had a ghost of a voice back, but decided against addressing the audience. Sara managed to be late, but compensated by sweeping onto the stage in an outrageous dress of red, white and blue to begin the concert. Her voice soared into the night and then she was gone, her part finished. Everyone relaxed, Anna noticed, and plunged happily into the rest of the music. Copland's *Fanfare for the Common Man* ended the main part of the concert, but Garrett's orchestration of "The Star-Spangled Banner" introduced the fireworks that arched and exploded high over downtown and Elliott Bay to the unanimous oohs and aahs of the assembled multitudes.

Anna felt tired and rather numb as she let herself into her house. To her astonishment Hal Corbett had offered to drive her home and chatted to her quite pleasantly, though when he began to speculate on the reasons for Garrett's decline in health over the course of the week, she had to stifle the urge to tell him to shut up. She retreated into preoccupied silence and listened gratefully as Hal's elderly Volvo wheezed back up the hill.

The air of the house was dead and stuffy after the hot day. She went around opening windows, then stood for a long while under a cooling shower. She crawled into bed in her coolest nightgown and let sleep take her.

The windows were open. No breeze stirred the curtains. Little pops, distant and nearby, punctuated the night as revelers saluted their country's birthday in backyards. Explosions ended Anna's first dreams. It took several minutes for the persistent knocking to penetrate her consciousness.

Sleepily she pulled on her robe and stumbled to her front door. "Who is it?" she said through the door, and then had to repeat it in a louder voice. She heard a muffled response calling her by name, and before she could think to tell herself not to, she opened the door.

On her threshold, Garrett leaned against the doorjamb, still in black pants and white dress shirt, opened at the neck, rolled back at the wrists.

"Hello, Anna," he said hoarsely.

"What are you doing here?"

"I had to see you." His eyes dropped to her robe and nightgown. "I'm sorry I woke you."

"You should be in bed, Garrett. What time is it?"

"I went home after I took Pamela to the airport. But I had to see you. Please let me come in. I won't stay long." He coughed once, wincing painfully.

"You sound awful, Garrett."

"I feel worse. I don't mean *ill*. Just about this whole thing. I need to talk to you."

"It's late. . . ." But even as she said it, she stepped back and let him in. She closed the door behind him, then walked carefully around him to turn on a light. "Do you want some tea," she asked him without looking at him. "Tea and honey's good for your throat, I think. I can't offer you anything stronger in it, I'm afraid."

"Tea would be very nice, Anna." His voice sounded different and she turned to look at him.

He was simply standing there in the middle of her tiny living room, looking at it, at her. "You know," he said, "I've never been inside before. This is really very nice, Anna. Very nice."

She'd furnished it in white wicker that seemed to fit its summer-cottage character. Bright, boldly colored cushions contrasted with the white. The small brick corner fireplace was obscured by a huge bouquet of white-and-yellow daisies. Framed posters decorated the pale yellow walls. An antique brass music stand stood in the large, paned front window that in daylight gave her a view of Lake Washington and the Cascade Mountains. "It really suits you."

"I found this deal on wicker. They're always having sales, you know...." Her voice twisted and died. His gaze was holding hers, and she felt the tug and pull of her need for him. "Oh, Garrett," she whispered, "why did you come?"

When he stepped toward her, she was powerless to stop him. Deliberately he raised his hands and placed them on either side of her head. He drank in her face, her eyes and then took her in a desperate, devastating kiss. She wanted to resist it. She put her hands up on his to pull herself away. But suddenly he was holding her close to him, molding his body to hers, drinking her in with his lips and tongue. And her arms went around him of their own accord.

When he released her mouth he still held her body to him. His neck was damp with sweat. He smelled like life itself. She realized her hands were under his shirt, caressing the strength of his back. Slowly she dropped them to her sides.

"Please go now," she whispered.

"I won't stay long. I just need to be with you. I need to see you. I've missed you, Anna."

"That's absurd," she began.

"No, it's not. You know it's not. We might have been a thousand miles apart all week long. That would have been easier. Easier than being in the same room with you day after day and not being able to talk to you, not able to touch you."

"Garrett, please. You're going to have to leave...."

He walked over to the couch instead and fell back into it. The wicker squeaked under his weight. He shifted a pillow to cradle his back and looked at her. "Not yet. Please, come sit here, Anna. Don't be silly about this. We've got to talk."

She folded her arms and looked down at him. "I'm not being silly."

He raised his hands and placed them squarely on his knees. "You're right. That's the wrong word. Sensible. Logical. Rational. Sane. Which is wonderful of you. Because it's everything I'm not at the moment. I've been through holy hell this week. I think you have, too. Only I've come out of it stark raving mad, and you're saner than ever." He leaned back as he spoke the last words. His eyes closed and his breathing deepened. For a moment Anna thought he'd fallen asleep. Quietly she slipped into the rocking chair opposite him and waited, wondering what to do next.

She was completely awake now and completely confused. For a week she'd watched him conduct, maneuver, charm, cajole, go through his entire repertoire. Most of the time she'd found it easy to distance herself from him, for this was a stranger, a public performer whose smile never quite reached his eyes. She'd watched him with the beautiful Pamela and seen their easy intimacy. She'd watched him with the dramatic Sara and seen the sparks fly. And not once had she allowed herself the luxury of self-pity, or self-indulgent tears. Because the Garrett she had watched all week hadn't been the Garrett who'd made love to her. When that Garrett, the private man who'd touched her body and soul during one searing night, had spoken to her that one time in the rehearsal room, it had been easy for her to close her ears and drive him out. When he'd asked for her help as his interpreter at the rehearsal, she'd been able to comply easily, for it was part of her role as concertmaster. But now he was sitting here in her living room, demanding to be dealt with.

She saw his neck muscles stiffen as he slowly raised his head. His eyes opened and he looked at her in protracted silence. "Do you know that you're beautiful," he said. It wasn't a question.

Anna folded her hands tightly in her lap and took the direct route. "Garrett, you're not making love to me. You can forget it. What happened happened. A one-night stand."

"Is that what it was for you?"

She didn't hesitate. "Yes. And for you, too."

A small, wry, rather sad grin tilted his mouth. "Oh. Well then. That settles everything." He studied his hands for a moment then looked back at her. "Except for why I can't sleep. Except for why I can't get you out of my head. Except for why I have to see you.

To tell you. To talk to you. To explain to you what—"

"Stop. Please. You don't need to explain anything to me."

"I think I do," he replied quietly. "I sure as hell do. And don't shake your head at me like that. I have to explain to you because what you think about me matters. Don't try to tell me that it doesn't. I know what this week has looked like. I sure know what it felt like to me. Like some kind of dreadful French farce. I kept waiting for a trap door to open up or a butler to fall out of the closet."

He drowned out her protests and they stopped talking at the same time. "Pamela Frost is . . ." he began. Then he stopped. "Well, you tell me what you think of her. I know you had lunch together."

Anna sighed and said resignedly, "I think she's beautiful and intelligent. She's very fond of you. She talked about you all during lunch. You make a great couple."

He sighed. "Pamela loves to talk. It's what she does best. We're friends, Anna. Not a 'couple.' Do you really believe anything was going on between us? You really think I would take you to my bed knowing she was arriving the next day to share the same bed? Do you really think that little of me?"

"It's none of my business," Anna replied in a voice the caught in her throat.

"The hell it isn't. Excuse me, but it is. Your business. I want it to be. I accused myself of being irresponsible the other day. But I'm not a cad. And I'm not a fool. At least not a complete and utter fool."

Neither spoke for a moment, then Anna murmured, "You didn't take me to bed. I came to you. I just figured my timing was rotten."

A hint of a smile glimmered in the corner of his mouth. "All your fault, eh? Pretty careless of you."

"Garrett..."

"Anna. I've known Pamela for the better part of eight years. We've never been lovers, despite what people will probably tell you. We've never exactly discouraged the rumors. But it's never been true. We're close friends. And that's all. I can only ask you to believe me."

"I believe you."

"You're lying."

"It doesn't mat—"

"It does matter. To me. Tell me this, what happened between us aside, do you think I would have allowed Pamela to come the same week Sara was scheduled, if we'd been lovers? Or do you think the three of us went to bed together?"

"I think I don't want to have this conversation."

He went on, his voice bleak and weary, breaking completely from time to time. "There's absolutely nothing left between Sara and me. Surely you could see that even in the rehearsal. If you'd seen us later in my office, you would know for certain. What we should have had was a grand and glorious affair and let it go at that. Marriage was a monumental error for us."

A silence yawned between them that Anna felt she had to fill. "She has a beautiful voice."

"She does. Yes, she does. But she's not a musician, Anna. Surely you could tell that. She has no real bond with her music. She's not a musician, despite her voice, which is exceptional. She's an actress, and not a very good one at that."

"And for this you threw her off?"

He looked at her in silence for a long, charged moment. "I forget, sometimes, how very young you are." He coughed and waved his hand in an erasing gesture. "That sounds patronizing. It's not meant to be. I mean that there's a lot of life you haven't met up with, that's all."

He seemed to hesitate, as if to collect his thoughts. Anna was torn between wanting to hear him out and wishing he would keep his secrets. His voice when he spoke was ragged and barely audible. "The situation between Sara and me was extremely complicated, extremely ugly and had little to do with music when you get right down to it."

Again he stopped completely. He seemed suddenly winded, exhausted. He hunched over with his elbows on his knees and looked at the floor. His voice was dead and flat when he said abruptly, "She aborted our child without telling me. I knew the marriage was in trouble from day one, but I had hopes that we could work it out. Especially when she got pregnant. But she didn't see it that way. She didn't want any impediments to her career. She didn't want to be encumbered. She didn't want—" He broke off completely and after a moment sighed again and went on. "Well, after that, there just wasn't any hope. Anything. Any peace at all between us until she left."

Anna was stunned. Soothing words came to her lips but she couldn't speak them for the sorrow she felt.

Finally she asked, "Why on earth did she come back?"

Garrett raised his head. He looked pale, drained, his eyes deep and dark under a frown. "I really didn't expect her to. But her agent made her honor the contract. For the work the fee was sizable. I agreed to cut the rehearsal time to a minimum, and she agreed to do the job. I don't know. Maybe she was curious to see how I was holding up." His gaze held hers. "Nobody knows, Anna, what I've just told you. Not Simon. Not Pamela. No one."

She looked at him steadily, her chest tightened with pain. "I don't know what to say," she said at last. "I'm sorry, Garrett."

Only his expression acknowledged her words. "When she really did leave last year, the void was enormous. It's odd how when there's a glimmer of a child, your mind leaps ahead with dreams and plans. Your life changes. Your view of yourself changes. And then it was over. And there was only this vast emptiness.

"I filled the void with music. I worked harder than I ever had. I began to pound the piano again. Simon encouraged me, of course. I began to compose again and even write some of it down. And slowly the emptiness began to fade. I wasn't going to let anything but music touch me again. I wasn't going to let anyone in."

He looked up then, his eyes full. "Not even you," he said softly. "But something happened."

She could tell he wanted her to come to him. She wanted it herself. She wanted to touch him and be touched by him. She wanted to give him comfort. But something held her back. She stayed in her chair. And he looked away again with a short sigh.

"What amazed me was all week how you didn't turn your back on me. Even though we never had a moment together, even though I couldn't tell you what was going on, it felt good just to know you were there. To know I could count on you whenever I needed you." He paused and seemed to force out the last, almost formal words. "I'm grateful, Anna. I couldn't have made it through the week without you."

"I was just doing my job."

Again the yearning look. "Please come sit here by me."

She shook her head. "No."

A moment passed in silence. "Have you heard anything I've said?"

"Everything. Every word. But if I come over there, I'll regret it forever. I have a job to do, Garrett. If we become lovers, I can't do my job anymore."

"We're already lovers, Anna. And you've done your job very well despite it."

She looked at him and saw him begin to smile. It made her tighten her voice. "Only because I told myself what happened that night didn't matter. Only because I promised myself I wouldn't think about it and that it wouldn't happen again."

He sobered and blinked. "I see."

"Even if everything you say is true..."

His eyebrows lifted. "If?"

"If. Even if I do, it wouldn't change anything. I felt used, Garrett. Deceived. I guess it was unintentional. But it hurt. If I didn't let it show, it's because I'm very good at hiding my feelings. All I want now is for you to let me finish out the summer in peace. Then I'll move on to another job."

"Do you think I'll give up that easily?"

"You don't have a choice. I'll quit."

He shook his head. "I didn't mean . . ." he began, and his voice died away. "Though I guess it comes to the same thing," he said quietly. He cradled his forehead in his hand. "I never meant to hurt you, Anna. Or deceive you. I just didn't expect...oh, hell. I can't put it into words. Feelings. What I feel for you."

"Don't say anything else, Garrett. Let's just end it here."

"Anna."

She stood up and said briskly, "I forgot about the tea. I'll make you some tea and then you can drive home. You need sleep. We've got a recital tomorrow. Remember? Honey or lemon?" she asked from the kitchen.

She made a long business of it—filling the kettle, measuring the tea into the tea ball, waiting for the water to boil, warming the pot, putting the pot, some honey and two mugs on a tray. She heard nothing from the other room. He hadn't followed her in. She had only the faintest hope he would leave before she returned. She wasn't sure she could face him again. His kiss was still hot on her lips, his voice, his sadness filled her heart. She wanted to touch him, hold him, gentle him, soothe him. And she wouldn't, couldn't let herself.

When she came back from the kitchen with the tray, she found him curled on his side amongst the bright cushions of her couch, sound asleep. His head was nestled on one hand. His long eyelashes curled on his cheek, softening the strong line of his nose. She put the tray down carefully on the table, found a sheet in her linen closet and covered him with it. She watched him sleeping for a moment, then turned out the light. On an impulse she didn't try to check, she leaned over in the darkness and pressed her lips against his damp and tousled hair.

Chapter Ten

At first it was like a dream: the feathery touch over her mouth, down her neck, across her shoulder, her name murmured in a gentle whisper, breath warm on her cheek. She smiled and stirred, holding the dream to her, wanting it to last. The kiss that began with such softness intensified and drew her out of sleep.

"Good morning," Garrett whispered, smiling into her surprised eyes.

She lay back against the pillow, pulled the sheet up and stared at him.

"We're going to have to quit spending the night together this way," he declared, arching back with a grimace. "My back feels as if it should belong to someone else. I wish it did." Then he went quite still.

He laid a hand against her cheek and she didn't move away from it. She felt him push back her mass of curly hair and watched his eyes roam over her face.

"I wanted to make sure before I left," he said quietly, "that you hadn't meant what you said. About ending this."

"I meant it." Her voice, untried, croaked.

"Your kiss told me it was only the beginning, not the end."

"I was asleep."

"You mean you weren't in control. Is that it?"

She looked at him.

"Try following your instincts, Anna. They're great instincts. Just for a change, don't try to think your way through this. Trust your feelings. Live the way you play music. The one won't cancel out the other." She looked away but his low voice persisted. "Try to trust me, as well. I know I haven't given you much reason to, but I've been in a very tough spot. If we lived other lives we'd have more time together, to get to know each other. I've wished a thousand times this last week that I could just stop everything, time itself, and just be with you. I want to know you. Everything about you."

His voice washed over her. Her face was still averted and he dropped his lips to her ear to whisper, "You may not want to hear this right now, but I think I may very well be falling in love with you. So if you won't consider your own feelings, consider mine and give me a chance to prove myself. Don't cut me out completely. Give us a little more time."

The bed rocked slightly as he shifted his weight from it. When she looked at him, he was standing on the floor beside her. "Go back to sleep. I'll pick you up at eleven so we can run through the recital before we perform."

"No."

"No?"

"You don't have to pick me up."

"Buses aren't very reliable on Sundays, Anna. I don't mind at all."

"But..."

"Until eleven, then. We'll go back to my house then walk up to the art museum."

My house. The words dropped like little bombs into Anna's brain. She felt the back of his fingers on her cheek. "Don't think about it. Just be ready at eleven. I know we need to work. And I promise you we *will* work."

She listened to him leave, lay back and tried to close eyes that refused to cooperate. The clock read just past seven, and it was raining lightly outside the window. She got up and pulled on a pair of warm-up pants and a long-sleeved T-shirt and let herself out of the house. Within minutes she'd walked the convenient steps she'd discovered at the end of her block all the way down to the lakeshore and was jogging slowly along the path, unaware of the gray blank of the water where it met the soft fog, unaware of the misty rain that came from all directions, aware only of the demands her body was making on her. Awakened by Garrett's caresses and kiss, her treacherous body ached for more.

For a moment she let herself imagine loving him. She let the feelings flood her and felt the release, the giving, the opening. She didn't know she stopped her jogging and was staring at the gray glassy water. When the tears began to run down her cheeks, she didn't know where they came from or why. Whether they were tears of sadness or joy, of fear or relief.

She had never before felt what she was feeling now. It was as if she were drawn to Garrett by an invisible thread, a string, a cord. It went beyond the physical attraction she felt for the man and the respect she felt for the artist. This was different. It was compounded by a desire just to be near him, by a need to learn every corner of his life, by a sympathy—or was it empathy?—or was it simply a deep concern for his well-being?

She began to move again, but at a walk not a trot, as she mulled over the quiet words he'd spoken in her ear that morning. "I think I may very well be falling in love with you."

Love. Well, what was that? Was it the name for the confusion of emotions that she was experiencing? Did it mean he was confused, as well? It was a startling thought. Anna had always considered Garrett to be sure of his every move, confident, precise. If he were in the same turmoil as she . . .

Could she say to him, I think I'm falling in love with you?

No! She couldn't commit herself that far, even if it was true. Because then what? The affair—odious word—would resume. They would steal moments together in the night, get gossiped about, ultimately break apart, and she would lose—again. No. She'd already lost everyone she'd ever loved. It was far safer not to love at all.

But she knew deep within herself that it was already too late. She could remember vividly how she'd felt that night on Bainbridge Island, stepping into his kitchen, stepping toward him in the night, offering herself, offering her love. And how readily he'd accepted it. Only to reject it the next morning.

Or had he really rejected it—and her? Was it possible that he'd been as surprised as she by what had happened? Had he needed time to think, to sort out his feelings? The time she was taking now...

But that was ridiculous. Garrett always knew exactly what he wanted.

She stopped again, clutching her head in her hands, totally confused. Her hair was damp with beaded mist, wisped into innumerable curls. He was the only one who had the answers to her questions. And she couldn't ask him, because even initiating a discussion of love was a declaration of sorts.

She turned in her tracks and forced herself to run hard back the way she'd come, listening not to her hectic thoughts but only to the squish of her soaked shoes on the wet pathway.

Garrett arrived promptly at eleven, and they worked from the moment they entered his house. He was in his usual preperformance state—taut, distracted, nervous—and promised to make up for it at dinner after the concert. Anna told him she'd consider the offer, which seemed to content him. As they walked up the hill through Volunteer Park toward the museum, Anna let him carry her violin, and when he claimed her hand on the steps that led from a quiet residential street up into the park itself, she didn't take it back.

The recital went well, considering their overflow audience at the Art Museum contained an inordinate number of families with young children. Everyone was smiling at the end.

Even Claire Terhune, who was making her way to the front, much to Anna's amazement. She was decked out in a long lavender skirt, white peasant blouse and a necklace of plum-sized porcelain beads.

"Aunt Claire!"

"Surprise!"

"I didn't know you ever went to concerts."

"It isn't often one's own niece is playing in one's backyard. So I strolled over to hear what you were up to."

"Aunt Claire, this is Garrett Downing. Garrett, this is Claire Terhune, my father's sister."

"I'm very pleased to meet you, Ms. Terhune," Garrett declared as he took her hand. "I called at your house one day when Anna first arrived, but you were engaged, if I remember, in fashioning a teapot."

He really was incredibly charming when he put his mind to it, Anna thought as she gazed at him.

"You've had a number of shows here in Seattle, haven't you?"

"Oh yes," Claire agreed, beaming from ear to ear. "A big one last December."

"You do wonderful work." Anna doubted very much if he'd ever laid eyes on Claire Terhune's pots.

"I'd return the compliment if I didn't have such a wooden ear. I must say you two looked very competent this afternoon. And everyone seemed to enjoy it."

Anna glanced at Garrett's face and saw a flicker of astonishment appear and vanish. "I'm glad you could come," he managed to say gracefully.

"I haven't seen Anna in such a long time. She calls me now and then and leaves messages on my tape, but there just never seems to be a moment. But, well, I just wondered—" she stopped, her hands clasped in front of her, her eyes darting between Anna to Garrett "—if you both could come over this afternoon. I'm having some friends in, artsy friends, you know, for tea or wine and cheese and things, and it would be lovely if you could come. There's even a musician or two in the bunch. This is such a small town, you probably know them."

Anna looked at Garrett and couldn't read his face. He was leaving the decision with her. "I can't speak for Garrett, Aunt Claire, but I'd be happy to come over."

She felt his hand lightly at the small of her back. "It sounds delightful, Ms. Terhune. I'd enjoy it."

"Oh, call me Claire. I hate all that Ms. stuff. So tiresome. Let me get a head start now and get things squared away. You come along when you're ready."

"You don't have to come," Anna said when the last of the audience had cleared the small courtyard.

"I know. But I'm fascinated by your family."

"She's all I have left," Anna protested.

"I know she is. Which makes her doubly fascinating. Not exactly sentimental, is she?"

"No, not exactly. She's got a good heart, though."

"Tell me about her."

"Well, she's my father's only sister. Younger than he by about ten years. Anyway, Aunt Claire never married and never had children. She has cats instead, several of them, whom she took in as strays. And she has her pottery. She's kind of a sixties person I guess. Or a beatnik. They were the fifties, weren't they? She just never changed."

"How well do you know her?"

"I lived with her from the time my father died until I went away to school. About eleven months. It really was very good of her. She really didn't want to deal with me."

Garrett looked puzzled. "Why on earth not? I don't exactly remember you as the juvenile-delinquent type."

Anna looked at him. They were walking along the shady road that led to the outer gates of Volunteer Park from the Art Museum. Opposite them on an island in the center of the drive was an old circular water tower, brick and substantial, unemployed for decades except as a lookout. On an impulse and to avoid answering his question, she said, "I haven't been up to the top in years. Would you go up with me?"

He followed the direction of her gaze up the enticingly ivied brick walls. "Only if you hold my hand. I'm afraid of heights."

The climb was easy and the view was tree-spangled but commanding as they went from window to window. Garrett pointed to the west, and Anna could see the cumulus clouds building above the Olympic Range. She could feel his breath on her neck in the warm, sweet prelude to a kiss, when a herd of small boys clambering into the chamber startled her away.

On terra firma once more, they strolled through the gates of the park and turned left. "So you haven't told me why your aunt didn't want you."

Anna sighed. This wasn't a topic she enjoyed. "I guess she didn't want to be saddled with the kind of burden she felt obligated to take care of."

"Do you really think she saw it that way?"

"Oh, she didn't say anything like that. But I mean there I was, this pathetic orphan with absolutely nowhere else to go. I didn't even have any close friends. Except for Simon. Dear Simon. Anyway, Aunt Claire was living here in this big house, and I'm sure she felt like she had to take me in."

Garrett was silent for a moment, then said, almost to himself, "Like a stray cat."

Anna heard him. "Like a stray cat. Exactly. That's exactly how I felt. Actually, I think it would have been better if I'd *been* a cat. She understands cats. Oh, no, that makes her sound terrible," Anna went on hastily. "She's not. She's precisely the way she seemed this afternoon. Eccentric, brash, forthright, a little crazy maybe. She's her own woman, and I admire that."

Anna felt his hand run softly up her back. "I've been wondering where you got that independent streak."

"Terhunes tend to make their own way in the world."

"They certainly do try. And they succeed," he added. "Look what you've accomplished in a mere quarter century. By the time you're my age you'll be filling concert halls all on your own."

She stopped in her tracks and stared at him. "What?"

He smiled down at her. "Just a prediction. You won't stay here long, Anna. You've told me yourself that you won't. I plan on keeping you here as long as I can, but you've got a future waiting for you. Especially with...well, it's only a question of time." A thought skittered through her mind: he was telling her that their love affair was bound to be brief, temporary. He was telling her he expected her to leave soon.

She pushed the thought away and addressed the other implication of his words. "You speak as if you're standing still, Garrett, when..."

"I've been here almost ten years. I probably should have left five years ago. But I was comfortable. Settled, for the first time in my life. I don't have your ambition, perhaps. Your drive. I certainly don't have your cool temperament."

The hot flush she felt under this unexpected barrage of praise made Anna feel anything but cool. She turned the focus from herself again. "Simon told me he thought you would become a legend in your own time."

"He said that?" She liked seeing him look that way, his eyes wide and surprised.

"In just about those words. Though he did say you'd have to move on."

"Ah. That's the hard part. I'm going to have to face it one of these years soon. Every year for the past five, I've thought, next year. Then suddenly it's next year and here I am. The problem is, I like it here. My house, the cottage on Bainbridge, my boat. The thought of growing old here doesn't disturb me in the least. The thought of going out and auditioning to take on a huge, money-making, world-famous orchestra in order to lead it to still greater heights strikes terror in my heart. I've built something rather good here and it's still growing. When I feel I can't give it any more, then I'll move on. Or retire. At least I'd have more time to sail. Or perhaps I'll take up something else. Write a book, maybe. *Twenty Years Behind the Baton* or some such. What do you think?"

She knew he was speaking half in jest, but she also heard the truth behind the lightness. "I think you can't be serious."

"I'm nearly forty, Anna."

She made a face. "Last time I heard, that was only a factor in careers like professional baseball. If you like, I could recite a list of elderly musicians and conductors who enjoyed productive lives long after they turned forty."

"I didn't say I was elderly." He was laughing, and she liked the sound.

"Oh? Sure sounded like it."

She felt his hand insinuate itself under the curls at her neck. "Maybe it's just that I'm jealous of your youth," he whispered.

She half turned to him. "Garrett, don't..."

"Don't what?"

"You get me all confused when you start talking like that."

"Like what?"

"I don't know. I'm not very good at this."

"Anna, don't be so hard on yourself."

She looked around, aware suddenly of where she was. "We're here," she squeaked. "Almost went past it."

Together they looked at the once-elegant old Victorian with its peeling paint, its wide front porch, the wooden swing hanging from rusted chains, the myriad flowers in their pots blooming chaotically in a riot of puce, yellow, red and violet. The orange cat sat on the porch railing with its tail in a comma, its eyes half closed, its front feet in two prim mounds in front of a splendid white ruff. "Are you sure you want to go through with this?" Anna asked. "You've just barely got your voice back."

"I wouldn't miss this for the world."

His hand lightly guided her elbow as they climbed the steps. Once inside, Claire took over the introductions. She'd been right. Garrett knew the musicians present and quite a few of the other guests. As he settled into a conversation with a harpsichord builder, Anna wandered off to the kitchen and helped herself to a glass of water, then busied herself passing around the cheese tray. To her amazement she recognized a woman seated in the rocking chair as a friend from high school days, now an actress with a local company.

The evening passed without Anna's having to talk to Garrett. She knew where he was every second of the time. She knew he had a long conversation with Claire on the front porch. She knew he had several glasses of wine and little else. She knew the instant his eyes found her, for she looked at him then and felt the now familiar pull. But she stayed away.

A delegation went out for Chinese food at eight, and by nine they were full of a variety of Oriental delights. And Anna was realizing how tired she was. She knew Garrett had to be exhausted. Again their eyes met and without a word to each other they bid their adieus and departed.

They walked in silence for some time, and then Garrett took her hand. The evening air was soft, just warm enough. "Were you avoiding me?"

"Yes."

"I thought so." He didn't speak again until they were outside his house. He turned to face her then in the twilight. He took her hands and kissed them one at a time. "Stay with me tonight," he whispered through her fingers.

It was so simple to say yes. Not to say anything. To go with him. But she pulled her hands away.

"Come in just for a little while," he urged gently. "I'm just not ready to let you go."

"If I come in, you know I'll stay."

"I do?" He smiled. "I'd say you'll decide that when the time comes."

"Garrett . . ."

"I like being with you, Anna. I want it to go on a little bit longer. Tomorrow is Monday again, and it's going to be another hectic week. Though with any luck at all it won't be as bad as last week. Nothing could be like last week," he added ruefully.

"But what you're really talking about is having me spend the night with you."

His eyes seemed to change color as he searched hers. "There's so much..." he murmured, then gently took up her hand again. "You know, it's odd. And I'm not sure how to put this. But I've been haunted this past week. I've wished that I'd been able to come to you as you did to me. Untouched. I wish that it had been my first time. That's what you've done to me."

She backed away, trying a practical approach. "Garrett, I'm no more prepared this week then I was last week. I feel like a fool, but I really didn't think that this..."

He put a finger against her lips and moved in to gentle an arm around her shoulders. "I'll take the responsibility," he told her softly, and added lightly as if reading her thoughts, "there's no harm in planning ahead, you know."

She let him steer her toward his house. It was close to dark now, though light lingered in the cloudless west. The house was dark and cool, its windows large rectangles of blue light and black shadow. Anna walked to the window beyond the grand piano and stood watching the horizon, the twinkle of the lights below on Lake Union and beyond on Queen Anne Hill. She felt his hand on her neck, caressing the tenderness beneath her hair. And she turned without a word, or a regret, into his embrace.

She awoke in his arms in the big brass bed as first light was glowing pale in the room. Contentedly she snuggled against his warmth and grunted softly as he tightened his hold on her without waking. A week ago she had awakened thus in his arms, and now again, after an interminable journey, she had found her way back home again. She could still reason that it was wrong, foolish, even crazy, but her body, her feelings wouldn't listen.

He'd taken his time last night, memorized every inch of her, taught her more about herself than she'd ever known. In her innocence she assumed her first experience had covered everything, but she'd been amazed last night to learn how wrong she was. With tenderness and skill he found what pleased her body, what teased, what emboldened and what released her passion. He entered her gently, gradually, driving her nearly to the edge as she discovered an intensity of joy she'd never known before.

The same joy washed over her as she moved against him now. She kissed the smooth firm skin next to his breast, trailing her fingers through the springy light brown hairs of his chest. She left a line of kisses along his collarbone and up his neck as she settled her body onto his and felt him awakening and quickening beneath her. She raised her head as she straddled him, looking down into his face as his long eyelashes fluttered and slowly raised. Then she pressed her mouth against his, tasting him, taking her time.

When they lay quietly again, still damp from their exertions, he said, "You learn fast, Ms. Terhune."

She chuckled, pleased by his pleasure. "I had a good teacher."

They lay in silence, relaxed but awakening to the fact that the morning was advancing.

"When does your day start, Garrett?"

"About half an hour ago, it seems."

"Seriously."

"Seriously I have to be at the office by nine. I'm also busy through lunch giving a lecture of sorts to the garden club at the Arboretum. And tonight . . ."

"Tonight we have an orchestra rehearsal. Dvořák and Ives and who?"

"A seventeenth-century French gem I uncovered about a year ago. I think we're giving it an American premier, but I'm not sure. Once that's out of the way, and we've taken the *Brandenburgs* to the hinterlands, we can get ready for Ivanov."

"Tell me how you convinced Ivanov to come. I mean besides being one of the world's greatest conductors?" Ivanov was in the world league, a giant among professional musicians. Along with Perlman and Stern, he was at the top of his field. Anna had been curious for weeks about his impending concert.

"Like so many things, we owe it to Simon, who knew him when. Oh, he's squeezing us in, I assure you, between stints in San Francisco and Chicago. But he's actually waiving a large chunk of his fee for our sakes. Otherwise we couldn't afford him."

Anna lay quietly against Garrett's shoulder and asked the question that had haunted her for days. "What if there isn't enough money, Garrett? What if the board decides the summer wasn't successful? What will happen?"

"What have you heard about all that?"

"Only that you'll be out of a job."

He snorted. "Ah, rumors," he said.

"You haven't shared the truth with me once. Should I know what's going on?"

"I'd have told you if I knew, Anna. So far, we've almost broken even. If we can hold our audience this summer, cover our traveling expenses when we take the orchestra to Wenatchee and Walla Walla, do well with Ivanov and—well, Pamela seems to think a record is a real possibility this fall. Public television is planning to broadcast Ivanov live, as well, which won't hurt, especially if it's good enough to send off to the affiliates around the country. We're not dead yet. But if it all falls apart, if everybody goes on vacation and nobody comes to the concerts, if the bubonic plague wipes out the woodwind section, if the bus to Walla Walla breaks down, then God knows. We'll probably join the ranks of a few other orchestras who've fought the good fight and gone down swinging." He touched her cheek. "But don't worry about it. Just play the music, sweetheart. I've hesitated to tell you that you're one reason we're doing so well. Didn't want it to go to your head."

"Heaven forbid. But I already know. I've even had a proposal."

"Someone I should be concerned about?"

"Well, he's only nine, but he's wild about me."

They chuckled together, and she wished they didn't have to move. Apparently, he felt the same because he made no effort to disentangle himself to get out of bed.

When he spoke again, his voice was low and gentle. "So how shall we play the week? Do you move in here or do we ignore each other or do we pick some middle road?"

"I was trying not to think about it."

"That's a start," he observed with an odd grin. Then he sighed. "Perhaps I should just make an announcement at the beginning of rehearsal tonight: the conductor and the concertmaster are having an affair, so kindly butt out."

A laugh bubbled up from somewhere, and Anna clung to him, shaking with giggles that very nearly verged on hysteria.

"Don't you think it would do the trick, eh?"

"I was trying to imagine Hal Corbett's face. He just decided to nominate me for membership in the human race because he figured out that due to last week's heavy competition I couldn't possibly be going to bed with you."

"Doesn't he know it's none of his business?" Garrett asked acidly.

"I get the feeling that in the orchestra everything is everybody's business. And I might say you have a really wild reputation in the ranks."

"No wonder you were so hard to get."

Anna felt a small part of her heart freeze over, and he grabbed her as she tried to roll away from him. "That didn't sound quite right, did it?" he asked softly. "I didn't mean it that way."

She made a try at careless laughter. "It's okay. All we've done is extend a one-night stand to a two-night stand."

"Right," he agreed after a second of silence threatened to last longer.

This time she escaped and disappeared into the bathroom, where she realized she had nothing to put on. She grabbed Garrett's robe off the hook, dashed back into the room and plucked her clothes from their various resting places on the floor and made a second escape. When she reemerged she knew what she had to say.

But he spoke first from where he was sitting up in his bed, a sheet of music on his knee. "You have a determined look on your face, Anna. What's the verdict this time?"

"Don't make fun of me."

"Anna."

"I feel a bit vulnerable right now. I'm going home. And I think we'd better steer clear this week. I'll see you at rehearsals, but I know we're both busy without trying to engineer time alone together."

He acknowledged the truth of her words with a frown. "May I at least call you?"

She took a deep breath. "I'd rather you didn't. I don't want to be a slave to the phone, wondering when you'll call or why you haven't called or whether I've missed your call."

He stood up and came toward her. She stood stock still and watched him. Naked, unselfconscious, he was lean but beautifully muscled, perfectly formed. He stopped just short of touching her. His gaze was locked on hers. "We don't really know what we want. That's it, isn't it? We're both scared of what might be happening.

"Yes, both of us," he went on. "I've made a mess out of my personal life so far, and it seems that you've simply avoided having one, for reasons I can only guess at. And yet, here we are, developing a relationship, as the current terminology would have it, and discovering that we like being together. We do fine as long as we stay in the present, don't we? But when we start talking about the future, even about later on today, we go all tense and awkward."

Suddenly he seemed to become aware of his situation. He blushed and turned away from her, found a pair of discarded jeans and pulled them on. He turned back with a sheepish grin. "I don't usually lecture in the nude."

Anna caught her lower lip in her teeth to keep it from trembling. "At least it holds one's attention."

Garrett held on to his grin for another moment, then crossed slowly to the window and stared out through the dogwood branches while Anna searched for a coherent thought. His voice was quiet as he spoke again, addressing the morning beyond his window. "I don't know if I can make any sense of what's going on, Anna. Not long ago you asked me what the most important thing in my life was. I answered music. But you started me thinking. Of course, music is my life. But as I tried to say earlier, I'm closing fast on forty. I lost a chance at a family recently, but the desire for one isn't dead. I'm settled here, for as long as I can make it work. While you . . . you're at the beginning of your life. I can't even think of asking you to give up any of it. You're going to go far, Anna. If you'd taken a different route, gone out for the international competitions for instance, you wouldn't even be here now. The more I hear you play, the more I know that your stay here is just a stopping place. You have something to give the world, and hiding in Seattle won't get the job done."

He was facing her now, his eyes glowing. "I want you to audition for Ivanov while he's here. I want him to hear you and advise you."

"Oh." She blinked. It had crossed her mind weeks ago, but only as a vague idea, not a definite plan. To cover up her confusion she said, "I'd rather hoped to at least talk to him."

"I think we can work out something more definite than that."

She managed a quiet "oh" again and stood looking at the carpet.

"But meantime, for as long as we can, I'd like to hold on to what we have. Even knowing that it can't go on."

Suddenly Anna understood what he'd been trying to tell her all along. He'd married Sara and admitted that his mistake was in not calling it quits at an affair. He was telling her that while he might want a family, he wasn't going to get permanently involved with somebody like Anna—somebody like Sara—who'd put her career above everything else. It made sense. He'd softened her with his tentative words of love just twenty-four hours before, and now, when she'd given herself again, he was telling her than an affair was all he could offer. But it was all she wanted, too, she told herself. Permanence wasn't something she'd even consider. They were in absolute agreement. She should smile. She tried, but it didn't feel quite right.

She took a deep, steadying breath. "What you want, then, is what we've got. A tidy little romance on the edges of real life. Everything in its place. While it's convenient. While it lasts."

His brow furrowed deeply as he looked at her. "You make it sound pretty terrible."

"I didn't mean to. I was just defining the terms. I wasn't objecting to them. Just making sure I understand you. I've fought you off and lost the battle, it seems. So now I'm just trying to make sense of the peace terms."

"Lord, Anna..."

"Before you start talking about love or something else irrelevant, just listen to me. If you want to continue this... whatever it is. Affair, all right. This affair. Then we're going to have to keep it strictly on the edge. I won't play games. I don't want looks or phone calls or hints or anything like that. When we work, you're you and I'm me and we're not an us at all." She meant every word, but her voice wouldn't work right. And there was a heavy heat behind her eyes that made her frown.

Garrett had retreated to the bed where he was sitting and looking at her curiously. "So according to your rules, when are we an 'us'?"

She shrugged. "Now. And the next time we can manage it safely."

"Oh." His voice tightened and chilled as he spoke. "All right. Let's see. How about next Sunday, then? I'll pick you up at eleven so we can drive up to Snoqualmie in good time for the recital. And afterwards we can have dinner at the inn and then... well, we'll see. But in between, we'll be strictly business. No billets-doux. No phone calls. No games, as you call them. And certainly no hungry looks. Does that meet with your approval?"

Anna had to admit it did. Sundays were for them, then, and the rest of the week would spin by as usual. It made perfect sense. Even though there was a hollowness in her chest she couldn't define.

Garrett was true to his word. He didn't quite ignore her completely, but he was distant, avoided her eyes and treated her precisely as he'd said he would, precisely as she thought she wanted to be treated. The days passed once more in a stream of music. And the days became weeks. On Sundays they played their afternoon recital, filling whatever hall in whatever town with beautiful sounds, filling the seats and aisles as their reputation as a duo grew. Afterward they were together, learning each other's secrets, touching each other's lives until Monday morning arrived once more.

Anna told herself she was happy. She had what she wanted. A wonderful relationship that didn't interfere with her musical life. A gentle lover who respected her need for solitude. Of course she was happy.

Chapter Eleven

By the middle of August the Northwest Symphony Orchestra was rehearsing for its final performance of the summer. They were opening with a Prokofiev suite, proceeding to a symphony by Shostakovich and ending with a performance of Beethoven's Violin Concerto by one of the world's leading violinists, Mikhail Ivanov.

Garrett returned after the break and tapped for attention. "I'm sure you have noted the Russian flavor of the program," he said with the ghost of a grin. "When I programmed it, I was hoping to make Mr. Ivanov feel at home. But it turns out I might have wasted the effort. He might not even be here for the first half of the program. In fact, we're fortunate that he's made time for one rehearsal. Tuesday night. He'll be en route to a series of concerts in California. The next time we see him will be when he walks on stage

Friday night to perform." There was an acidity and a tightness to Garrett's voice that disturbed Anna. She watched him carefully and noticed that he didn't look at her once.

"You've worked hard," he continued. "We're all ready for a break." He paused. "What I'm about to say now isn't much of a way to say thank-you. But I know some of you have already heard quite a few rumors. Everyone knows the smaller orchestras of this country are in trouble. And we haven't escaped. The Summer Festival was as successful as I'd hope or dreamed. For that I am very indebted to all of you. We've had generally good houses, excellent publicity, good coverage . . . but." He sighed. "There's always a 'but.'

"Several things have to happen before we can come back together this fall. We have to have a smash with Ivanov. A full house. A crackerjack television-radio simulcast. And a recording contract. You are aware that Pamela Frost has been here several times this summer. She's taken some good tapes of us and done her best to sell us as an item. She's bringing several people with her next week to listen to our grand finale. If they have an offer, it won't be our finale. It'll be the beginning of a new year."

Anna sat listening to the man who was her lover. The man who'd said so little about any of this during the precious hours they'd lain in bed together. Who'd said almost nothing about it when they'd worked together, traveled together, talked together. Of course, she'd been very aware of Pamela and her visits and stepped aside while the woman dominated Garrett's time and concentration. She'd known the record was a possibility. But she hadn't really realized its full importance. She sat listening.

"I thought you ought to know where we stand, all of you. I'd like to think we can perform an excellent concert. But we can't do it without hard work." He stopped for a moment and then picked up the heavy score on the music stand before him.

"You may like to think that the Beethoven Violin Concerto is an old, familiar friend." He smiled. "Most of you know I'm very suspicious of the familiar. It's a devilishly difficult work. The solo is a beast, but the orchestra's part is fully as important and has more than its share of horrors. Anyway, Ivanov is going to give us a run for our money. I've studied his last recording of the piece, and it's very different in significant ways from any other I've ever heard. What he'll expect from us I honestly don't know. I've tried to get an answer from him and failed." Garrett came to a halt for a moment.

"After a lot of soul searching I've decided to rehearse the piece around the solo. I've rethought a lot of the music and I know exactly what I want the orchestra to sound like. So, I've decided against asking the concertmaster to fill in on the solo."

He looked straight at her for the first time as he added, "Anna has a sound all her own, and I don't want her sound and interpretation confusing the issue. We have to concentrate on ourselves as an orchestra and be ready for Ivanov."

She returned his look with something like amazement until he glanced away. She'd told him she'd been practicing it and couldn't wait to play it. He might have warned her not to bother. She dropped her gaze to the music on her stand and felt her color rise with her anger.

The rehearsal was interminable, and Garrett disappeared immediately afterward. He never stayed around to chat. He continued to keep his distance from his musicians, just as he had from the beginning. It was only when they were alone together that Anna felt the warmth he was capable of. And now she was thinking over his pronouncements and wondering if she really even knew him at all.

The last weeks had swept her along in a haze of work and—what? Love? Passion? Fulfillment? She didn't know what to call it. She and Garrett on a Sunday afternoon, playing music, eating dinner, talking endlessly, making love, talking again, sleeping in each other's arms. There were the other times together, stolen times when he'd taken her out in his car, then turned the wheel over to her, teaching her to drive, teaching her to love the feel of the responsive, energetic silver Jaguar. There had even been one crazy Saturday two weeks before when he'd helped her buy a car.

Even so, there were few enough times that she could still recall each one separately, remembering what they'd talked about, the exact words they'd said. She could remember each separate time they'd made love, what it was like, what she'd learned, what she'd felt.

But none of that helped her now as she sat after the rehearsal, wiping the rosin from the burnished wood of her instrument. She considered her options. She could follow him, perhaps even find him in his office. She could call him on the phone later that night and demand to know why he hadn't confided in her, or at least why he hadn't told her not to practice the Beethoven solo. Or she could— "Hey, Anna, why so glum?"

She turned to see Tom MacMahon bending toward her over her music stand. Jan, his fiancée was close behind him. Her mind scampered. "Oh, Tom. Nothing, I guess. I was just thinking about all the 'good' news. I guess I didn't know we were in such desperate straits."

"Oh, hell," said Tom. "What else is new? It's like this every year now. Hanging by a thread. Then some local corporation comes through or we get some kind of grant and we eat again for another few months. If I remember correctly, the old maestro gave us the same cheerful little pep talk at the end of last season. Then he turned around and fired about two dozen of us. Those lucky few of us who were left pulled up our bootstraps and cinched in our belts, and here we are. Want to join us for a beer or something? How's that snazzy little Ford of yours?"

Anna joined her friends and was glad of it. Talking helped. Everyone had ideas about finding money or jobs or both. Tom said seriously that even if the orchestra closed down, they could keep the quartet going and get plenty of jobs. Jan mentioned teaching. They all agreed glumly it would be hard to pay the rent without taking on extra nonmusical jobs. Anna said little, but no one seemed to notice.

Her mind wandered back to Garrett. She had to see him, yet she wasn't sure how. Calling him, going to his house broke all the rules she'd set for herself to follow. They were rules that had worked so far. She and Garrett had been able to maintain their dual lives.

But their lives had changed this week. She had no more one-to-one rehearsals with him. Their last sonata recital had been the previous Sunday. They'd performed in a Mercer Island school auditorium to a packed house, eaten dinner in a Bellingham restaurant and parted company in the small hours of Monday morning without knowing when they'd next get together. And now, driving home in the warm darkness, in the very car he'd helped her choose, she began to feel that it had already ended; she just hadn't been informed. She went to bed angry with herself and with him for their mutual silence.

The following day Anna didn't cross Garrett's path all day. By five o'clock she was exhausted enough not to care about the consequences and found her way to his office.

His secretary was gone and his door was shut. She knocked and despite the silence within tried the knob. The door swung open and revealed Garrett hunched at his desk, staring down at a piece of paper.

"I need to talk to you, Garrett. I know your time is valuable and all that, but..."

"Shut the door, Anna," he said in a strange, husky voice.

She gritted her teeth, but obeyed then turned to face him. "I'm really mad," she began again. "I feel left out in the cold. I mean about yesterday. You could have warned me about the solo. You knew I was spending a lot of time on it."

He looked up at her wearily. "You'll play it some day. I honestly wasn't absolutely sure how I was going to rehearse it until yesterday." His voice was colorless and sounded as if it didn't want to work.

"But that doesn't explain," she persisted, "why you haven't told me more about the whole situation."

"What situation?"

"Garrett! I'm talking about the orchestra."

He covered his eyes with his hands. "I can't do this," he said softly.

"What's wrong?"

He looked up at her and his eyes were full. "Sit down," he whispered hoarsely.

She stayed where she was, fully alarmed now. "What is it?"

"This." He lifted the paper, an ordinary sheet of stationery. "This arrived about a half hour ago. It's Simon." She waited, not daring to breathe. "He's dead, Anna. A stroke they think. I wish there were a better way..."

Her chest contracted and she felt she would disappear in her pain.

But he was there, holding her against him, stroking her hair, whispering through the roaring in her head. "I'm all right," she murmured at last, her voice muffled against his chest.

He kept his hands on her shoulders and looked into her face. "I'm so sorry," he said softly.

"What happened?"

He hugged her close again as he talked. "He died in his sleep Sunday night. They've buried him there. He was with what was left of his family. It's what he would have wanted."

A thought crept in and she looked into Garrett's face to voice it. "Was he sick when he left?"

Garrett drew her to the couch by the wall and sat down with her, cradling her against his chest. "Yes," he admitted softly. "He didn't want me to tell you. You or anyone. I know I should have told you. Prepared you somehow. But he really believed he would come back. He planned to come back to hear Ivanov."

"He seemed older, but all right...." she said in a small voice.

"He'd been failing all year, Anna," Garrett said gently. "Longer than that, really. I wasn't sure what to do. He was such a good friend on the one hand. But as a musician, it was so difficult.... He came to me last winter and said he was retiring, to save me the trouble of firing him. He said it with that funny laugh of his. We talked for hours. He told me about his prognosis and how he wanted to go back to Europe and Israel and tie up the loose ends of his life."

She sat thinking over what she knew of Simon. All the times she'd spent with him. The letters she hadn't written him during the past few years. The last lunch. The postcard she'd received. She looked up into Garrett's face. "Why didn't he tell me?"

"I don't know, sweetheart."

"There was so much I could have said to him, if I'd..."

"He knew. He knew you loved him."

She was crying again, great heart-shredding sobs that left her weak. He sat with her, comforting her, until her grief subsided. And then they talked. She was barely aware that he took her to a small restaurant until he was ordering a meal.

There was a long silence between them. Anna wasn't sure what she'd eaten, only that it had been chicken in a delicious sauce. A mug of decaf steamed in front of her now. She felt drained.

"There is one more thing you should know. One other thing that Simon told me before he left." Garrett took her hand. "I wish he'd told you. It would make this easier."

"What?"

"Simon wanted you to have his violin, Anna."

She caught her breath. "Garrett, it's a Stradivarius."

"I know. One in a million."

"I can't..." She'd taken her hand away and was clenching it with the other.

"You'll have to, Anna. Someday. It's yours. It's in the orchestra vault. You know he'd want you to play it. I know he'd want you to play it tonight."

Anna felt the tears well up as she wondered at this extraordinary gift. Simon had treasured his Strad since the twenties. He'd smuggled it out of Germany in the thirties. He'd have protected it with his life. And now...

Garrett was talking quietly. "Do you remember that day we climbed the water tower at Volunteer Park and went to your aunt's party? I was talking about your future. I started to tell you about the violin that day, because I know it will make a difference. Not that your instrument isn't a fine one. It is. But you deserve the finest."

"I don't know how I could play it," she said in a small voice.

"You will. A violin has to be played. It's not built to be hidden away in a vault. And who is to play it now, if not you, Anna?"

"I'd be afraid for it all the time," she protested. "It's priceless."

He nodded and took her hand again, chafing it with his own. "You'd best leave it in the vault when you're not playing it. Keep yours at home to practice."

She looked at him and shook her head.

"Give it time," he said. "Think about it. Think about what Simon wanted."

They left the restaurant, and he drove her back to her car, pulling in next to it. It was nearly eleven and a misty rain was falling.

"Thank you," Anna said. Her head ached and she felt as if all her tears had gathered there behind her eyes.

Garrett opened her car door for her. "So how's the car?"

"Okay. No problems."

"Good. Do you think you can drive home? You must be tired. I can take you, or..."

"I'm fine." She eased into the driver's seat. He stood with his hands on top of the door.

"Do you want to be alone tonight?"

She looked over at him. The streetlight's glare illuminated his shoulder and left his face in shadow. "I think so. I think it's better ended, don't you?"

He drew a deep breath and released it slowly before he spoke. "I guess I'd rather end it, yes, than keep going the way we were, the way it was."

"I guess I feel the same way. But..."

"But?"

"I don't regret anything, Garrett. I don't want you to think that."

"I'm glad." He reached over and touched her cheek in a soft caress. "I thought it would be enough. But I was wrong. I guess I'm not as good as you at drawing the lines." He withdrew his touch. "But I'm glad you have no regrets. I would hate it if you did."

The kiss was sweet. The tenderest of goodbyes. His lips were as soft as his last smile as he closed her car door. "Keep in touch," he said at the end. "I'll be at all your concerts this weekend. And then we'll face the tiger next week."

Ivanov was the tiger. He didn't really look like one, but looks, Anna knew, were deceiving. He was of average height, and stoutly built with a barrel chest. He carried a full head of gray curls and a proudly hooked nose. He walked on the stage Tuesday night as if he owned it, said a few inaudible words to Garrett, acknowledged the orchestra with a nod and waited silently for his entrance. Garrett stood on the podium for a full half minute, as if gathering his thoughts. Then he raised his baton and they began.

The rehearsal seemed endless and excruciating. Ivanov's tempos were unexpected, his approach to the music quite different from what Garrett had anticipated. Garrett tried his best to accommodate him, but the orchestra floundered in spots, despite everyone's serious efforts to avoid it. Before he left, the soloist had a few more words for the conductor's ear alone, and then he'd taken himself off.

Garrett kept the orchestra in their seats while he stood silently on the podium, and then he'd attacked with all his verbal weapons. Not a single section escaped his wrath. The orchestra members, Anna knew, were thoroughly demoralized by the news of Simon's death. Garrett had exhorted them to pull together and informed them that Friday's concert, the grand finale of the summer, would be dedicated to Simon's memory. And now, as he concluded his biting critique, he reminded them of that fact once more and left the room.

"Go away," was the answer to her knock.

She opened the door anyway.

"This is becoming a habit," he observed acidly. "I'd like you to turn around and leave, Anna. Leave me alone. Talking about it won't solve the problem."

"I'd like to hear about the problem," she insisted.

"You already did. We made hash of it downstairs. Ivanov could barely restrain himself from laughing aloud. He told me he would be claiming his full fee, that the orchestra didn't deserve a break. Didn't deserve to survive."

Anna felt her anger rise. "He said that?"

"In just about those words."

"And you turned around and took it out on us."

"Damn right I did."

"Then whatever happens, you're absolved completely."

"Far from it. It'll probably cost me my job in the end. But I won't go down without a fight."

"You'll do better with us on your side."

"Anna, we've had this argument before. But I can't change the facts. We're out of time, and if we pay off Ivanov, we're out of funds, as well. Of course, if we play Friday the way we played tonight, we'll also be a laughingstock."

"It wasn't that bad, Garrett. The Prokofiev is damned good, and..."

"We have different perspectives, you and I."

"What can I say that will make you understand?"

"Nothing. I do understand. Just do your job, Anna. And let me do mine."

"With pleasure," she said, and slammed out of his office. He'd closed her out completely. It was as if he didn't want her to exist. She'd ached to see him smile, even laugh at himself. She'd yearned to touch him, hold him, listen to his fears, his ideas. But he'd held her off with a steely look and a bitter voice.

"It's over, over, over," she repeated to herself as she drove home, almost comfortable with the car now, almost comfortable with her familiar route up and down the hills of the city. A summer to remember. An affair to forget. He obviously couldn't even bear the sight of her. His last show of tenderness had been for Simon's sake, out of pity for her grief. He didn't care. He'd seduced her, used her, and now it was over.

All through the night she tossed and turned, looking at the summer from every angle. Most painful to recall were the early times, the happiest times, somehow, when they were learning about each other, when they were alone, intimate, communicating. They'd been rare times, but wonderful. The end had really started near the beginning of it all, when they'd laid down the rules for the relationship. She'd set the limits, and he'd agreed. It had all seemed right at the time. It had all seemed reasonable and civilized. But something had slipped out of place during the weeks that followed. And now it had all broken down. Go away, he'd told her. Go do your job and leave me alone.

All the next day Anna worked at home. Her commitment to the Northwest Symphony was nearly at an end. No one had mentioned extending her contract. Indeed, the entire orchestra would be without contracts come September. In retrospect she realized how much had not been said at that first interview when she'd been hired. She hadn't asked. The board had not offered any information. And now she'd have to start over again. Applying for auditions, preparing a tape, traveling, surviving. But she realized it wasn't so terrifying now. She'd already survived so much. She'd start with San Francisco, ask if they had an opening and go from there. If worse came to worst, she'd stay in Seattle—no, she realized in the same instant. Anything but that. Coming home hadn't worked out very well. She'd leave. She'd go anywhere rather than chance meeting Garrett unexpectedly on the street.

Alone in her tiny house on the day of the concert, Anna looked out her window at the thick, moist air that obscured the lake and the mountains beyond and practiced her music. To the pale yellow walls and empty wicker sofa she played the entire Beethoven Violin Concerto—the soloist's part Garrett had forbidden her to play. Every note flowed from her memory to her fingers.

She played with it, had fun with it, relishing every sound. She imitated Ivanov and his erratic approach, his hesitant entrances, his headlong tempos. And she echoed her memories of Simon's playing during the languid slow movement. In the sounds of her own instrument, she heard Simon's exquisite Stradivarius. She hadn't played it yet, but she knew the time was coming. It was no longer an appalling thought, but a fitting tribute to the man who had given her so much.

As she finished the last note, she curtsied laughingly to the silence of her empty living room and realized that it was her first laughter in a long while. It felt good. Her music had won again. She was free of Garrett Downing. After tonight he would be behind her, part of her past.

At six o'clock she put on the new sleeveless black concert gown she had found unexpectedly on a sale rack of a tiny downtown dress shop. Mindful that she should look her best for a live broadcast, Anna was inspired to replace the trusty black skirts that she'd worn for concerts since graduate school. The new one was a bit daring—showing off rather than camouflaging her figure. She examined herself in the mirror and studied the V that threatened to plunge between her breasts. Not too low, she decided, but almost. The skirt was eased from the hips and the silky lightweight fabric swirled about her ankles.

As was her custom on concert nights, Anna arrived well ahead of time. She was excited, nervous but excited.

She started down the narrow corridor toward the musicians' locker room, her dress shushing softly around her legs. There was a lone man in white shirtsleeves pacing at the shadowy far end of the opposite hall. She hesitated for a moment, then realized that it was Garrett. She could have gone on past, ignored him, pretended he didn't exist. But she knew very well he was horribly nervous and tense. She'd been with him during some of his worst moments that summer and learned how vulnerable he was to his fears. She couldn't not say something.

He heard her approach and whirled. "What?"

"I just wanted to say that I hope it goes well," she said softly.

He stood very still. The light was dim at the end of the hall, the red exit light nearly winning out over a sixty-watt bulb overhead. She couldn't read his face, but she could feel his tension. She moved closer.

His voice stopped her. "Have you got that section of yours together, do you think?"

She bit her lip. "As well as I can."

She could see the color rising in his throat. "No one promised it would be easy."

"No. I didn't want it that way." She lifted her hands. She didn't want to argue. "Garrett, listen, I just wanted to say, if I don't get the chance, that I've enjoyed it."

"Enjoyed it," he echoed.

"Yes. The summer. Everything." It sounded absurd, but it had to be said. And one never knew who was coming down the hall, around the corner. "Thank you."

"You're welcome," he said, using the same formal tone she had. "You sound as if you're leaving right away."

"I don't really know. But I expect I'll be leaving soon."

"Are you coming to the reception afterwards? For Ivanov, if he deigns to show. At the president's house."

"I was invited, but I'm not sure . . ."

"Do come," he urged, and looked away. "It'll give you a chance to talk to Ivanov, anyway, set up a meeting with him."

"I'm not sure I want to."

"Don't be foolish," he said with the ghost of his old, intimate tone. "He'll know what you need to do. I can't advise you. I . . . w-well," he stammered, and looked away again.

She did it without thinking. Just reached up on her toes and pressed a kiss against his freshly shaven cheek. He responded by grabbing her into a sudden hug that stole her breath, it was so fierce and tight. She felt his cheek press down on her head, felt his arms strong around her, felt his heart drumming, felt his hard, vibrant body fold her into itself. He didn't say a word. And in silence he released her, then turned without meeting her eyes and went through the exit door. She heard him take the first few steps, then the heavy door crashed shut, leaving her alone.

The next time she saw him he was taking his bow under the lights. She'd made her entrance, noted that the house was gratifyingly full, tuned the orchestra and adjusted herself to the bright lights demanded by the television cameras. He came on as he always did, rapidly, with all his powers concentrated, completely under control, all business. The scene in the corridor might not have happened. His hair was carefully combed back, the ruffles at his breast and wrist were starched and radiantly white against the jet black of his formal jacket. His white bow tie floated like a small valiant bird at his throat.

He stepped onto the podium, waited for silence, then turned to face his audience. "This performance," he said in his clear, carrying baritone, "is dedicated to the finest musician and the finest human being I have ever known. Simon Weil. He graced this stage for twenty years and only last May played his last concert here. He loved this, his adopted city, and he loved this orchestra with a passion that inspired all of us. We will miss him."

When he turned back, he looked directly at Anna, moved his gaze significantly over the entire orchestra, lifted his baton and with it shaped the opening notes of Prokofiev's music.

The first half went well. Garrett gave them all a nodding smile as he left the podium. The audience loudly approved before dispersing to enjoy the intermission.

Anna was seated again for the second half, and the orchestra was tuned. They were all waiting for Garrett and Ivanov to come onstage for the Beethoven concerto. Preoccupied with the music she was about to play, Anna gradually became aware that quite a few minutes had passed. She knew they were on a tight schedule because of the broadcast. The break was lasting too long, but then she decided that Ivanov was in some sort of interview that television relished. The rustling expectant hush of the audience had become a general, impatient noise; the orchestra members shifted in their chairs and whispered.

Suddenly, a hand tapped Anna on the shoulder. She turned to see Mr. Johnston, the orchestra manager, bending over her.

"Please come backstage," he whispered.

Anna rose automatically, not allowing her mind to work, and avoided the curious looks of her fellow musicians as she followed in the man's wake through the large door at the side of the stage.

Garrett stood against the far wall of the dim corridor, his arms folded across his chest, somber gray eyes on her alone. Anna knew immediately what was happening.

"Where is Ivanov?"

"In Portland, Oregon," was the flat reply.

"That's ridiculous."

"That's what I said. But it appears that Seattle-Tacoma is fogged in and so they sent the plane with Ivanov on it back to Portland. When the fog raises a bit, they'll send the plane back to Sea-Tac. But we don't know when that will be. He may be on his way now; he may get here at midnight. This sort of thing usually only happens in the winter," he added in a voice that was clipped and colorless.

"Oh, Lord," Anna breathed. "What about the telecast?"

A short balding man she hadn't seen before stepped forward. A one-eared headphone made him look like a lopsided man from Mars. "They're running out of things to talk about," he said with a grimace. "We have got to get this show on the road."

There was a pause, then Garrett asked her softly, "Can you play it?"

Anna met his eyes and without hesitation said, "Yes, I can."

"I should have rehearsed you," he admitted with a shadow of a grin.

"Yes, you probably should have. But I've been working on it."

"I've sent Johnston up for the music."

"I don't need it."

"Don't be absurd, Anna."

"I'm not being absurd. I memorized it my last year in school. I played it yesterday from memory." She couldn't help adding, "Some of us plan ahead." She wanted to see him smile. He did. She continued, "I know it. But I'm warning you, I won't be Ivanov. I'll just be me."

Garrett nodded, his eyes on her face, his face awash with strange emotions. "That'll be enough," he said, and brushed her shoulder with his hand.

"Do we have time to get Simon's violin? I'd like to play it now."

He smiled wonderfully and nodded. "Tell Johnston to get it. I'll go out there and keep them occupied." The small bald Martian muttered something into his headset, then pointed significantly at Garrett, ordering him out the door.

Anna heard the audience gradually hush as she stood behind the door, waiting, gathering the music in her head. Mr. Johnston was back in moments with the Stradivarius, and she tuned it as she listened to Garrett's words.

"Ladies and gentlemen, I apologize for this delay. I have just been informed that Mr. Ivanov's plane is being held in Portland, Oregon, because of local fog." There was a general murmur that rose then hushed in a wave. "I assure you that there will be no change in our program. Our own concertmaster, Anna Terhune, a former student, incidentally, of our late colleague Simon Weil, will be performing the solo." She heard him begin the applause.

Anna took a deep breath and walked out on the stage. She met Garrett's steady gaze and let it draw her up the long path to the front. As if in a dream she saw him take her hand and raise it briefly to his lips. He smiled into her eyes, and she felt strength and confidence flow into her. She turned and took her bow.

The audience grew still. The musicians awaited the conductor's sign. A moment of pure silence, and then the orchestra began. Anna stood perfectly still, letting the magnificent sounds of the lengthy introduction wash over her. The great music engulfed every sense, encompassed every emotion. At precisely the right moment Anna raised her violin to her chin and began to play.

Chapter Twelve

Anna returned to the world as the storm of applause hit her broadside. She opened her eyes to see the entire audience standing as one body. There were whistles and shouts of *"Brava"* and *"Bravissima"* above the din. Anna turned slightly to see Garrett taking a stride toward her. She was stunned to see tears in his eyes and his face luminous with happiness. Taking care not to include the precious violin in his embrace, he hugged her closely to him while the audience redoubled its noise.

She bowed again as Garrett turned to bring the orchestra to its feet, and they, too, applauded Anna. She began to laugh aloud as the noise reached an absurd level and her feelings could no longer be expressed in a smile.

The applause faded as the audience became aware of a portly figure walking down the aisle. He quickly climbed the steps at the side of the stage and walked gravely over to Anna. A cameraman jockeyed his awkward equipment into position as Mikhail Ivanov captured Anna's small slender hand in his large paw and kissed it feelingly.

The applause began to build anew, but Ivanov raised his hands above his head for silence. When the orchestra and the audience were all seated and Ivanov stood with Garrett on one side and Anna, her hand firmly clasped, on the other, he spoke in his heavily accented bass.

"My English not so good, but I must speak," he began. "You people of Seattle, you have not been disappointed tonight I think. You came to hear this old Ivanov fellow and you hear, instead, this young woman here. This young woman whom I have never met before. This young genius from I do not know where. I have not heard the beginning of the concerto, but have come in during the slow movement. My plane is late. I am running fast. I think what am I to do if they started. But I cannot stop her. I must hear this to the end. And soon I think the world will hear her."

Merry applause greeted his words, and Anna felt she might burst. "I know the television is on me, and I want to say that I never miss a chance to be on the television. If I could be here, I would be here. But I know if I was here, we might not know about this young woman yet.

"And her orchestra," he half turned, gesturing. "A fine job, all of them. I owe them and you a concert, I believe. Not tonight. Tonight is hers. But I will come back soonest. It will be my gift to you and my pleasure."

Ivanov led Anna off the stage, then made her go back again to take another bow. When she came off again she was greeted by a man with eager round eyes and a microphone. Behind him was another man with a camera, and before she knew what had happened she was in the middle of an interview. She was aware that Garrett was in the background, and that Ivanov and he were talking, and that they were joined by Pamela Frost and two other men. Five minutes after it was over, she couldn't remember how she'd answered the interviewer's inane questions.

What followed next was utter confusion. The orchestra as a body rallied around her, while several journalists and more than a few intrepid members of the audience tried to reach her. Ivanov intervened, handling the media with the aplomb of an experienced pro, and led her out of the crowd. He kept her in tow the rest of the evening, in fact, taking her to the reception that was supposed to be in his honor, introducing her to his own entourage, sketching out the next few months of her life.

At the reception Anna was received like royalty. Pam Frost and her people were there talking records. A corporate executive was talking money for the orchestra. The board was talking a long-term contract for Anna. Garrett was there and seemed to be watching her carefully. She wanted to take him by the arm and drag him off somewhere quiet where she could talk to him, where she could think. But it was impossible. Gradually she realized his predictions were coming true. She had, in fact, played for Ivanov. And Ivanov was, in fact, advising her. Advising her to be in New York by September. Advising her to work with him. Advising her...

It was three before she got home. Her phone woke her up at eight. And again at eight-fifteen. She unplugged it and dozed on until nine. It rang twenty times between nine and eleven.

It would all die down, she told herself as she pulled on pants and a T-shirt. But still echoing in her ears was Ivanov's heavily accented voice telling her on the phone at nine that morning, "First September, I want you in New York. Come ready to play. I will listen. We will work. I will get you an audience of agents who will kill to sell you. I know people, Anna."

At ten-thirty, the manager of the San Francisco Symphony had phoned her. He'd heard part of the broadcast and wanted to know if she was available to talk. At ten forty-five, the Portland Symphony called. Portland PBS had picked up the simulcast, and the PSO wanted to know what her schedule looked like for the coming season.

At eleven she simply fled her house. Down to the lake in the sun. The sun after five days of rain and fog. If they'd had sun instead of fog yesterday, Anna mused, then she would still be just the same Anna. The season would be over and she would be wondering what to do next. Instead of—she laughed aloud at herself. She was still the same. She was wondering what to do next. The only difference was she had a future to walk into instead of just a past to walk away from.

In a trance she went down the path toward Seward Park. All she'd done was her job. She'd simply stepped in when she was needed. True, she'd enjoyed every minute of it. She'd absolutely relished every note. And she'd carried the orchestra with her all the way. Garrett had . . .

Garrett.

She plunged her hand into her pocket and found a quarter. She trotted to a nearby convenience store, waited while a sweaty cyclist made a call, then dialed the number. She let it ring twenty times before she hung up. She'd never called him before. Not one time. And now when she mustered her nerve, he had the gall to be away.

Maybe he was running. Maybe he was with Pamela. Maybe he was at the airport. Maybe at the office. Saturday morning. But an unusual Saturday morning. The Festival was officially over. There must be lots to tidy up.

Anna went back to the phone and dialed Garrett's office.

His secretary answered.

"Susan, this is Anna."

"I've tried to call you three times."

"I'm not home. Everyone else was calling me."

"How does it feel to be famous?"

"Weird. Is Garrett there?" she asked with her heart in her mouth.

"Yes, sort of. He's in with the board and Ms. Frost and her boss. Negotiations. They have to catch a plane for L.A. in an hour. He said not to disturb him. But I'm sure that he'd make an exception for you."

"It's all right." Just the thought of breaking in on him was enough to make Anna lose her nerve. She didn't want to talk to him with everyone listening. "I'll catch him later."

"Shall I tell him you called?"

"Don't bother. Will he be home later, do you know?"

"He told me he was going from the airport over to his house on Bainbridge. You know his number over there?" Anna wrote it down.

"Say, Anna. I didn't tell you how great you were. The phone's been ringing off the hook. Can you come in Monday to answer some of the messages?"

Anna extricated herself from the conversation with a vague promise to come by on Monday. And she continued walking. It was nearly eleven o'clock and becoming hot. Sails darted across Lake Washington in the brisk breeze. Beyond the trees, the snowy tops of the Cascades gleamed, defying summer.

But Anna noticed nothing. Her thoughts were fixed on one person. She had looked forward to this moment, she remembered, when she would no longer have to see him, no longer have to work with him, no longer have to wonder if what she said sounded correct and neutral, no longer have to turn her eyes away when she knew she'd looked at him too long.

"You love him, dammit." She said the words softly to herself. She knew she'd loved him all along. She'd never said the words. She'd been too careful for that. Too wary of committing herself. Too concerned for her career. Too concerned for what people might think. Too terrified she might actually have to depend on something as chancy as another human being.

But as careful as she'd been, as wary and as scared, her heart had ignored her head. Her heart had quietly learned to love both man and music and wound them up together into her life. Her love for him had made her music possible, she realized. For what else had she expressed last night but love? Love was the wellspring of her art.

She remembered the morning after they had first made love. She'd awakened alone in his bed to hear his music washing over her. She'd lain listening, wanting him to come back to her. She'd listened to the music, but she hadn't heard. She hadn't understood what he was telling her.

She remembered all the times they had played together, just the two of them. All the practicing, the six recitals. The suspension of all else but pure sound. Pure love, she knew now. Early on when they couldn't even speak two words to each other, they had their music. And those afternoons they performed, knowing they would soon spend precious hours in each other's arms, they had entwined their art, melded their voices, in a kind of rapture of anticipation.

And then it had ended. Or had it? The recitals had ended, and then there'd been the rush toward the end of the season. Garrett was loaded down with rehearsals, meetings, demands and deadlines, burdens he hadn't dared share with her. She had been the one to say it was over. He had only agreed with her that they couldn't keep on with it the way things were. He'd left it at that, closing her out, just as she had closed him out.

Anna walked up the long hill toward her house. She couldn't have told anyone when she'd turned around and headed home. But she had arrived at a decision. She couldn't leave without going to him, without seeing him, without asking, without telling.

She ran into her house, packed a duffel bag with a small lunch and a change of clothes and started up her car. A half hour later she was on the deck of the Seattle-Winslow ferry, the sun on her back, the wind in her hair and the hoarse cry of the ever-hungry gulls ringing in her ears. All that was missing was Garrett, holding her the way he had that day as they steamed toward Kingston on their way to Port Gamble. She rested her folded arms on the rail and closed her eyes. The absolute worst that could happen was that he would say he didn't want her. He would tell her to go. He would tell her he didn't love her. But even as she thought it, she was certain that he did. That he'd backed away from her because he loved her. That he'd agreed to the terms of their relationship because he loved her. That he'd hated them because he loved her. His love had shone in his eyes last night, had been in that quick mad embrace he'd given her when she'd found him alone in the corridor before the concert.

It seemed like forever until the orange-coated man waved her car out of the ferry's hold. She bumped down the ramp, climbed the hill to the stop sign, and turned left. She recognized the place where she and Garrett had struggled with the tire that cold, rainy night. A thousand years ago. A lifetime ago.

She nearly missed the turnoff. His mailbox carried no name, just a number. The driveway was barely visible between the trees. The underbrush was dense, obscuring the house completely until she was suddenly upon it. Beyond the house she could see open blue sky. She remembered the house backed up to the water. She was trembling slightly when she climbed out of her car. Then she realized that his car wasn't there. He wasn't there.

The silence of the place struck her then. Not silence exactly, but quiet sounds so different from the sounds of Seattle. Wind in the trees. Bird songs. The rhythmic shushing of waves. A small distant clanging sound.

She went around to the back of the house and followed broad steps to the water. She heard the ferry hooting around the edge of the bay, out of sight. Garrett's sleek white sloop lay tethered to its buoys. It swung around, trying to nose into the wind, and she read its name *Intermezzo*. The term for a quiet musical interlude. A musician's day off. She smiled. It explained the sunburned nose he'd sported on occasion. A rope clacked against the sloop's aluminum mast. Slap, slap, in a rhythm that countered that of the waves and the wind. She let her eyes sweep past the boat across the water to the skyline of Seattle, where strange spires rose in the sun and danced in the heat. Far away. Anna breathed in the smells and felt calmer than she had in weeks.

After a while she climbed the steps Garrett had set into the hill, back up to the car to fetch her duffel and the book she'd been meaning to start all summer. For once, she had plenty of time. She'd wait for him.

Just as she came around the corner of the house she heard a car. She stood very still as it came into the clearing and stopped, skidding a bit on the soft gravel. She couldn't see his face because of the reflection. His door opened slowly and he stood up.

"Hi," she said.

"Hello," he answered. Then one side of his mouth lifted. "You'll never guess where I've been."

"To the airport."

"There, too. Then I came here. Then I couldn't stand it anymore, Anna. And I couldn't bear to use the phone. I had to see you. So I went back to Seattle."

She caught her lip in her teeth. "I wasn't home."

"I know."

"Why did you want to see me?"

He searched her eyes. "Perhaps you should go first."

She straightened her spine and lifted her chin. "Well, Garrett, I need your help. I don't know what to do."

He looked away for a moment. She could see it wasn't what he wanted to hear. She smiled to herself, enjoying the moment. "There are a lot of decisions to make, and I can't seem to decide what to do next."

His voice was gruff. "I'm not sure I can advise you, Anna."

"Why not?"

"Because I'm prejudiced."

She looked at his face and wrinkled her nose. "Don't think I'm any good, do you?"

Within a breath she was in his arms, the air being squeezed out of her. His kiss was hungry, deep, joyous.

She broke away then and held his face between her hands. "I love you, and if you really want to get rid of me, you're going to have to put me on the plane yourself."

"I was afraid you'd already left. I've been such a fool, Anna." He hugged her to him. "Say it again," he whispered. She repeated the simple words, and he echoed them again and again.

She pressed her lips against his neck and reached for him as he bent his head. The kiss lasted until she thought her legs would give way. But he swept her up into his arms with a grunt. He stopped at the door. "Oh, damn," he said. "It's locked. So much for romance." She giggled as he set her on her feet and trotted back to his car for the keys.

Hours later they lay in each other's arms, deep in the quietness of the afternoon.

"So tell me about all these decisions you have to make," Garrett said quietly, his hand tracing the line of her arm, up and down.

"Well, Ivanov wants me to go to New York. He's full of ideas, just like you said he'd be. San Francisco still wants me. Portland wants to know if I'm available. And the Philharmonic," she improvised. "Lenny Bernstein called me personally. And Boston was very embarrassed about letting me get away, and..."

"Northwest wants you to stay on this next year," he interjected.

"That means the orchestra is still alive?"

He grinned. "It seems so. The board thinks that on the basis of what we did this summer and the interest and support that's come in since last night, they can keep us going for another year. And Pam's company is committed to a record. As long as you're featured on one side. They hope to record some time next month and have it out by Christmas."

Anna was very quiet as her mind churned through the facts. Then she sat up and looked at him full in the face. "You're telling me that everything rests on what happened last night. On me, in fact."

"Am I?"

"It sure sounds like it."

"You see, I'll resort to blackmail to keep you here."

"Blackmail?"

"If you won't stay just because I want you to, I'll have to convince you that seventy-five souls will starve if you leave."

"Garrett, you never asked me to stay because of you."

"I was hoping you'd decide on your own."

"You've been telling me to go, to get on with my career. You've been telling me you didn't want to hold me back."

"I was lying. I didn't really know I was lying. I thought I was being, I don't know, noble or altruistic or something. When I was really scared to death of what I was feeling for you. I'd worked through so much after Sara left. I thought I knew what I wanted. Then you came along and threw everything into total chaos. I wanted what was best for you and I somehow worked out that I wasn't part of it.

"But suddenly I knew I wasn't going to be able to live without you. When I realized you weren't going to come storming into my office anymore complaining and telling me how to do my job, explaining your theory of friendship and the difference between nice agreeable criticism and . . ."

"Tell me one thing, Garrett."

"Anything."

"Tell me what would be happening now if everything had gone as scheduled last night. As you'd predicted. The weather was clear. Ivanov's plane had landed on time. We'd slaughtered the Beethoven as he fiddled away. And the orchestra had gone up in smoke. Pam had taken her boss home to L.A. and it was all over."

He lay back and closed his eyes. She watched his chest rise and fall. His voice was low and quiet. "I'd never have let you go home alone last night. But if for some reason I had, I would have found you this morning to tell you that whatever happened, I wanted to be with you. We'd plan out our future together, and wherever one of us found work, the other would go and do whatever he or she could do." He opened his eyes and looked into hers. "Because I love you, Anna. I don't want to let you go. I did once. And I almost let it happen again. But I just can't do it. You're my life, Anna."

"How long?" she asked when she found her voice.

"How long have I loved you?" He slipped one of his hands behind his head and cocked an eyebrow at her. "If truth were told, probably since you were seventeen."

She chuckled. "You're kidding."

"No, I don't think I am. I remember watching you then, and thinking, oh, if she were just a little older. And then, just when you got older and I thought perhaps I could make a move without being arrested, you wrote me a polite letter asking me to write recommendations for you to this and such university. I thought seriously about sabotaging your chances, telling them what a miserable little brat you were."

She poked him in the ribs. "You wrote good ones. Look where they got me."

"No one took my word for anything back then. Where you got, you got on your own, miss."

"Humph. Well, I guess I've loved you that long, too. It wasn't love then, though. Not really."

"You told me not long ago you hated me in those days."

"I lied. I dreaded meeting you because you made me so nervous. I never knew what you were going to say. My palms got all sweaty. I preferred you in the abstract. I memorized all your numbers—license, phone, address. That kind of thing. Other girls had movie stars and rock stars. I had you."

He lay back and laughed delightedly, a wonderful sound to Anna's ears. "I can't believe this," he said.

"I thought it was just a girl's fantasy. Until I met you again."

"So you didn't really come back because of me."

"More in spite of you."

"Ouch."

"To show off perhaps."

"I'll accept that."

"But what happened after that..."

"I wasn't too tactful, was I?"

"No, you weren't."

"What if you'd succumbed that first night..."

"No way."

"You do prefer to do things your way, I've noticed."

"Whenever possible."

"Me, too. What are we going to do about that?"

"Compromise."

"Compromise?"

"I'll stay on, as your concertmaster, if you let me hyphenate."

"Hyphenate?"

"A quaint custom. Popular in England, I believe. Armstrong-Jones, Burke-White."

"I don't know," he said slowly. "I'm rather traditional. Old-fashioned."

"Hmm," she answered, and planted a kiss just below his right nipple.

His hand delved into her hair. "Probably because I'm so much older than you."

"You old fogy," she murmured, moving her hand down the smooth taut skin of his belly.

"Hey," he said.

"Not so old," she said.

* * * * *

COMING NEXT MONTH

#583 TAMING NATASHA—Nora Roberts
Natasha Stanislaski was a pussycat with Spence Kimball's little girl, but to Spence himself she was as ornery as a caged tiger. Would some cautious loving sheath her claws and free her heart from captivity?

#584 WILLING PARTNERS—Tracy Sinclair
Taking up residence in the fabled Dunsmuir mansion, wedding the handsome Dunsmuir heir and assuming instant "motherhood" surpassed secretary Jessica Lawrence's wildest dreams. But had Blade Dunsmuir wooed her for money . . . or love?

#585 PRIVATE WAGERS—Betsy Johnson
Rugged Steven Merrick deemed JoAnna Stowe a mere bit of fluff—until the incredibly close quarters of a grueling motorcycle trek revealed her fortitude *and* her womanly form, severely straining *his* manly stamina!

#586 A GUILTY PASSION—Laurey Bright
Ethan Ryland condemned his stepbrother's widow for her husband's untimely death. Still, he was reluctantly, obsessively drawn to the fragile-looking Celeste . . . and he feared she shared his damnable passion.

#587 HOOPS—Patricia McLinn
Though urged to give teamwork the old college try, marble-cool professor Carolyn Trent and casual coach C. J. Draper soon collided in a stubborn tug-of-war between duty . . . and desire.

#588 SUMMER'S FREEDOM—Ruth Wind
Brawny Joel Summer had gently liberated man-shy Maggie Henderson . . . body and soul. But could her love unchain him from the dark, secret past that shadowed their sunlit days of loving?

AVAILABLE THIS MONTH:

#577 FALLEN ANGEL
Debbie Macomber

#578 FATHER KNOWS BEST
Kayla Daniels

#579 HEARTSTRINGS
Grace Pendleton

#580 LEAN ON ME
Carolyn Seabaugh

#581 THE PERFECT CLOWN
Carole McElhaney

#582 THE LYON AND THE LAMB
Pat Warren